WHAT IF . . .

ACKNOWLEDGEMENTS

A huge thank you to all friends and family who have read my stories and given me feedback and helpful comments, which have encouraged me to keep going. Thanks also to Richard Stockwell and crew, who thought my work was publishable.

WHAT IF . . . ?

Alan Mills

ARTHUR H. STOCKWELL LTD
Torrs Park, Ilfracombe, Devon, EX34 8BA
Established 1898
www.ahstockwell.co.uk

© *Alan Mills, 2021*
First published in Great Britain, 2021

The moral rights of the author have been asserted.

*All rights reserved.
No part of this publication may be reproduced
or transmitted in any form or by any means,
electronic or mechanical, including photocopy,
recording, or any information storage and
retrieval system, without permission
in writing from the copyright holder.*

*British Library Cataloguing-in-Publication Data.
A catalogue record for this book is available
from the British Library.*

*This is a work of fiction. Names, characters and incidents are the
product of the author's imagination and any resemblance to actual
persons, living or dead, is purely coincidental.*

ISBN 978-0-7223-5078-2
*Printed in Great Britain by
Arthur H. Stockwell Ltd
Torrs Park   Ilfracombe
Devon EX34 8BA*

HEAVEN FORBID

Having just come off my diet, which had lasted a month, I was feeling quite excited at the thought of being invited out to dinner. My tastebuds wanted to be revitalised.

"Where did you say we were going?" I asked my wife.

"Eileen and John's" was her reply.

'Oh, my God!' I thought. 'The last time we went there I am sure we had roadkill – well, it certainly tasted like it.'

"Do we have to go?" I asked.

"Why?" was the reply.

When I explained, my dear wife just laughed and said that I was being ridiculous. I did not think it at all funny – in fact, I recall it quite well.

After the initial front-door greeting of "Hello. It's been ages. When was the last time?" we were shown into the lounge, where we were offered drinks. Their house was a large rambling building with the kitchen and bathroom along a hallway leading into the rear garden. After a mouthful or two of my beer I excused myself to go to the bathroom. Along the hall I went, and as I got nearer to the bathroom I realised that the smell coming from the kitchen was not of lamb, beef or pork, but of God only knows what. It smelt bloody awful.

When I arrived back in the lounge, my dear wife said, "OK, love?"

"Fine," I said, but I made a face in her direction.

Eileen and John then excused themselves to put the final touches to the meal.

My wife then said, "What's the matter?"

I said, "Go to the loo, and have a sniff as you pass the kitchen. Then you will know what I mean."

Shortly after, John appeared and asked us to come through to the dining room. This we did.

"What would you like to drink with your meal?" asked John.

"Well, what are we having?" I enquired.

"As a starter we have butternut and hedgehog soup, followed by a three-bird roast," said John.

"Ah [quickly thinking], soup I find a little filling," I said.

"Don't be silly – you love soup," my wife emphasised.

At that moment I wanted to divorce her – no doubts.

"Well, I will try a little," I said. "And I will just have water to drink as I am driving," I continued.

"No you are not – I am," insisted my wife.

Can you divorce someone twice!

Eileen joined us as the soup was being served and said, "Just mind the spikes."

Just mind the spikes! I ask you! This was not from a packet or tin – this was acquired from the corner of the garden!

"The three-bird roast sounds a nice idea," I said.

"Yes – my own recipe," said Eileen proudly.

I was intrigued, and asked, "What are the three birds?" And with bated breath I waited for the answer.

"Blackbird, sparrow and rook," she said.

I glanced at my wife (who was still my wife for a little longer) and just smiled.

All I could add was "Lovely! And will we have to be careful of the feathers?"

At this point my wife gave me an almighty kick in the shin under the table.

Coming to the end of the main course, I think I realised what spitting feathers meant. My plate had more on it when I finished than it had before I started!

"Lovely! I am full," I said. (I lied.)

"Oh, you must try some pudding," said John.

"I am sure I could not eat another thing," I pleaded.

"Nonsense – it's crushed holly berries and ice cream," Eileen confirmed.

'Wonderful!' I thought. 'The general hospital is not too far away, and if we drive fast I might get my stomach pumped out before I die!'

"Well, you won't have to worry tonight as we are having a fish-and-chip supper," my wife said. Continuing, she added, "So you will be a happy chappie, I think."

Fish and chips at Eileen and John's? Is that possible?

"Might that be goldfish and chips?" I enquired, only to be told, "Don't be silly."

I wondered what might be for pudding.

TEA FOR TWO

Another day with the rain pouring down and the wind howling outside! I was pleased to be in, but after five days it would be so nice to stretch my legs. I was feeling rather cooped up in the house, like a caged animal, eager to get out and explore. Perhaps tomorrow might bring some respite from this dreadful spell of weather.

My first thought upon waking was could I hear rain against the window? All seemed quiet on the wind-and-rain front, so I eagerly got up to see. Whilst outside was wet, there was no rain falling, so I became quite excited at the possibility of actually going for a walk – a long walk.

Since retiring some ten years or so ago, I made a point of getting regular exercise, and a brisk walk allowed me to do just that. It was not something though that came easily to me, like it did my dear wife. She used to love to walk and walk and walk. For her it became a social event as well – meeting people along the route, most of them with similar interests. Sadly though, no longer! My wife passed away some five years ago, having suffered from dementia.

I then started this debate with myself: Where would I go?

'Oh, just get out and walk,' I urged myself, so I did.

Trethorne Gardens were situated approximately a mile away, and a stroll around there would stretch the legs. Making the most of being out, I viewed the plants and bushes and smiled to myself. It never ceases to amaze me that, despite the wind and rain, nature carries on regardless. Many others were out taking advantage of the rainless day too, and judging by the looks on their faces they were pleased to be out in the fresh air.

After an hour or so I began to think of some refreshment and I looked forward to a pot of tea in the café back at the entrance to the gardens. I would make it my next stop. Whilst there were several people out walking, not many ventured inside for refreshments.

'Strange!' I thought.

With tea in hand I found a table and settled down, but for some reason I soon found myself glancing across the café and daydreaming. What about I cannot recall – obviously nothing important. I do though find people-watching quite fascinating. Staring right at the person or persons, I find I can begin to build a picture of the character behind the face. Of course I never know if my thoughts are accurate, but it's fun just thinking about it. When I came back into focus, though, I found myself drawn to one lady in particular. She had arrived at the counter for a cup of tea, and she looked very sad – desolate in fact and completely bewildered. She seemed to have so much on her mind that she was struggling to find any money to pay. I really felt very sorry for her – why, I cannot say. Rather than watch her fumble for coins in her pocket or purse, I stepped forward and offered to pay for her tea. To save herself from any further embarrassment she nodded acceptance of the offer, and added a thank you. I then invited her to sit with me, which hesitantly she did.

In a split second I realised that there was something unusual about her. She was a very smart, attractive lady, but a lady who had been shocked and hurt by something. I was keen to understand the story behind the sadness, if it was forthcoming. It was none of my business really, but I was interested nevertheless. Although what followed I had partly anticipated, I felt no joy in being partially right.

"Thank you for taking pity on me at the counter like that," she said.

"No problem," I answered. Not sure what to say next, I blurted out, "You do seem in some distress, if you don't mind me saying."

It took a minute or so for her to answer. Then she said, "You could most certainly say that. My husband has just kicked me out."

"Oh, my God! I am so sorry" is all I could say. I was not expecting that.

Over the course of the next few minutes or so her story unfolded.

"We had a Christmas party at our house two days ago. My husband, Brian, became more than amorous with a much younger guest – a secretary at my husband's office. Her name is Lana. She spent most of the night flashing most of her assets, encouraged by my husband, and both were aided by plenty of alcohol. I was so upset. The following morning when I challenged him about his behaviour he admitted that he and Lana had been having an affair. He added that it had been going on for many months, and if I didn't like it, tough, I could leave. I am not the sort to take things lying down – I lost my cool and a fierce argument ensued. I told him he was an absolute bastard behaving so badly in front of our friends and humiliating me in the process. At that point he hit me, twice. 'I am off to play golf,' he said. 'I don't expect you to be here when I get back.' I just grabbed a coat and the doorkey, although I am not sure why. With absolutely no idea where I would end up, I started walking and found myself here."

"Well, that is not a nice situation to find yourself in. Look – would you like something to eat?" I enquired. "I need something, and perhaps you might care to join me."

"Under the circumstances," she said, "yes, I would like that. But I don't know you from Adam," she added.

"No, but we can do the introductions later," I offered. "I only live about twenty minutes away, and – who knows? – some food and a drink might start to cheer you up a little. Regardless of the situation, I find a glass of wine, of either colour, can work wonders."

Arriving home, two glasses were poured whilst I prepared something to eat.

"So where do you go from here?" I enquired.

"I really am not sure. I guess I need time to reflect on my life and to come to terms with what has happened," she reasoned. "I suppose I need at some stage to try to retrieve some of my things and some money. There is no way I want to go back there to all the lies and deceit."

"Well, I am Chris, and if there's anything that I can do to help please say."

"You are very kind. I am Daniella and I am pleased to meet you." A brief smile followed. My act of kindness triggered several tears at that moment. "Do you think in a minute I could make a call?" she asked.

"Sure," I said.

I indicated the way to the bedroom, where there was an extension enabling a private conversation to take place. She made her way to the bedroom, where she plucked up the courage to call her husband and arrange collection of some things, hopefully the following morning. She told me that was agreed, but she wouldn't go back there until he was at work, after 9.30 a.m.

During the evening she offloaded her complete story, which I think made her feel better.

"I had had doubts about Brian for some time. Sudden nights away here and trips away there although previously his job never required going away at all! Six months ago some friends dropped a few hints and fears of what might be going on. I visited his office two days ago, to surprise him, and this was where I first came across Lana. 'Very high maintenance!' was my first thought. Short skirt, skimpy top, heavily made-up, nails polished and very sultry-looking. She seemed very embarrassed to meet me, but, to her credit, carried off the brief encounter well.

"When Brian appeared on the scene, rather red-faced, 'What are you doing here?' was all he could say.

"'I thought to pop in and surprise you,' I offered.

"'Well, I have to prepare some figures for an important meeting over lunch,' he said.

"So with that I left. Curiosity though got the better of me, and before driving away from the car park I decided to sit in my car and see what would happen next. Ten minutes later he and the lovely Lana rushed out of the office to his car. I decided to follow them. Three miles down the road they pulled into a restaurant next to a Holiday Express Motel. Tears started streaming down my face, and I could so easily have driven home, but I decided once again to wait and see what happened next. Forty-five minutes or so later the pair reappeared and ran towards the motel. At home that night I challenged Brian, who took exception to being followed.

"I was very annoyed and yelled, 'You always said you couldn't shag on a full stomach.'

"With that I received a smack in the face, knocking me to the floor. It was at this point that I realised the rumours were true and the end of my marriage was imminent.

"The following evening was the Christmas do, so I decided that I would stay and try to enjoy that with my friends. But he and Lana were behaving in such a blatant manner that it shocked many of our other guests."

More tears followed – probably tears of relief that she had told the story. I put a consoling arm around Daniella and suggested she needed something to eat and a good night's rest. In the morning she could make some decisions.

"One last point," I said: "I have a spare bedroom and you are welcome to use it for as long as you wish."

With that she smiled, nodded and, following a simple meal, settled down to relax as best she could.

Following a good night's rest Daniella enjoyed coffee and toast and decided what she was going to do.

"Would you drive me to my house so I could collect some things?" she asked.

"Of course," I replied.

However, before I could add anything else she gingerly asked if she could stay a few more nights whilst she sorted out what would be her new life. Not wishing to put anyone on the streets in their time of trouble, I agreed. In fact I was pleased she decided to stay.

Ten Years Later

Well, Daniella stayed, not only for a few extra days, but, well, she is still here. She went through a tough time divorcing Brian, and starting her life again. However, we in a way found each other through her mess and married some seven years ago. We are both very happy. We never forget our meeting in the café at the gardens. My instincts on that occasion were proved to be spot on, although Daniella has since told me not to get too thoughtful when I see other people with a sad look on their face.

Brain and Lana's relationship did not last. Some twelve months after his divorce she went off one morning and never came back. I often wonder why.

SEDUCTION ACROSS THE GARDEN

Glancing out of the bedroom and across the garden, I couldn't help but see a lovely-looking youngish lady dressed in just a bra and . . . That in fact is all I could see, but I wanted to see more. Who wouldn't?

My friend's house was in the middle of a terrace of five, whereas the house across the garden was at the end of a terrace of four. We were approximately sixty feet away from each other. It was eight o'clock in the morning and I guess that the young lady was getting herself ready for work. Curiosity, though, was mounting; so was the heightened sense of excitement. I mean the thought of what I could not see was too much to consider, especially at that time of the morning!

It was a silly thought, but what if I walked around the corner sometime to see if this lady was outside? ('More likely at the weekend,' I thought.) Maybe she'd be washing her car or cutting the grass. Yes, what if . . . ? Walking was not my favourite hobby, but I could get excited over 400 yards.

That evening I went to bed at about eleven o'clock, and as I went to pull my curtains across I glanced again out of the window and saw a soft light on in the window across the garden. There too was the lady, pulling her curtains across in preparation for sleep. I of course did not know the name of this lady, so in my mind I called her Beauty.

My visit was coming to an end. I would be driving back to the West Country the following day. However, in my mind I started to plan my next visit so I could hopefully continue my relationship, which was, I realise, a ridiculous thought.

Four Months Later

After a tiring drive back to my friend's house in the Midlands, followed by a lovely evening meal, I decided to have an early night. I climbed the stairs and opened the bedroom door and went instinctively to pull the curtains across. It was approximately 10.30 p.m., and there she was, Beauty, doing coincidentally the same thing – pulling her curtains across too.

'Perhaps,' I thought, 'this visit I will meet her.'

It was Saturday morning, and a sunny morning too. Following breakfast and a read of the morning paper I decided that it would be good to go for a walk and then try the local pub for a pint and maybe some lunch. Of course my walk would have to start with a stroll past the house across the garden.

"You're back quick," my friend said as I opened the door after about fifteen minutes.

"Yes, but you know walking is not my favorite hobby," I joked. "Perhaps I'll go again later," I said.

"Fine. Come and do some shopping with us now and walk later on," suggested my friend.

Sunday came and once again we were blessed with a fine, sunny day. A walk to the pub seemed an attractive proposal, so at about midday off I went. As I turned the corner excitement took over – there she was, washing her Ford Focus.

'Now what do I do or say?' I asked myself. 'Nothing, of course.'

It was that simple. She was probably a married lady or at least engaged to a young man who would show her a good time.

"Good morning," I said as I approached. "You've chosen a nice day for it. You can come and do mine after if you like," I added jokingly, nodding towards the car.

What a chat-up line that was!

She stopped and smiled and just said, "I've nearly finished, and I am not wanting to do any more, thank you."

I mentioned where I was staying and she melted into conversation. After a few moments I said that I was going to the pub for a lunchtime drink. To my utter surprise she said, "Oh, I might see you shortly. I was thinking of doing the same."

'Oh, be still, my beating heart,' I thought.

I strolled to the pub with excited anticipation.

Ten minutes or so later the bar door rattled and in walked a lady – the lady from across the garden.

"Hello again," I said. "Would you like a drink?"

"Oh, a G & T would be nice, thank you," she said.

We found a quiet table and chatted non-stop. The lady, I discovered, was not married and did not have a current boyfriend. She was a part-time solicitor.

After an hour or so we walked back towards the estate and we agreed that it had been an enjoyable lunchtime.

As we reached her house I completely out of the blue said, "How about continuing this tomorrow evening?"

And to my amazement she said, "Fine – say seven thirty?"

Gobsmacked, I nodded, and walked around the corner. Beauty was now Carla – at last I had a real name to call her.

Carla and I enjoyed a lovely meal the following evening, and considering our age difference I found it really enjoyable.

Dropping her back to her house, I was asked, "Would you like to come in for a coffee?"

Surprised, I readily agreed. I mean it was not one of the hardest questions I have ever had to answer.

Our chat continued over coffee in her lounge, where I asked, "If you are a part-time solicitor, what else do you do? Or am I being nosy?"

"Ah, now that is a question – you may not like the answer to it though," she suggested. Cheekily she then added, "Pub lunch tomorrow and I'll tell you. I mean it is a bank holiday, so no work!"

A few miles out of town we found a village pub and settled for a table outside in the garden.

After a glass of wine and a light lunch Carla said, "Can I say that I have enjoyed your company over the past few days."

"The feeling is mutual," I eagerly agreed.

"OK, now to the question you asked me yesterday. Let me

be completely honest: up until three months ago I was an escort, or, as some call it, a call girl," she stated. There was a stunned silence, and then she continued: "I was a solicitor in the mornings and an escort in the afternoons and evenings. That, though, came to an end when I was diagnosed with sepsis about four months or so ago," she explained. "Now I have a limited time to live, barring a miracle," Carla continued.

My natural reaction was to say, "You are joking, right?" But this was serious.

"Look – sepsis comes when your immune system overreacts to an infection or injury. In my case I had a bad fall down some steps. When my speech started to become slurred the people in A & E thought that I had been drinking, but it was early in the morning. Other symptoms followed much later, at which time I was diagnosed with advanced sepsis. Oh, and I have a life expectancy of approximately six months." She smiled as she completed her story, and I thought how bravely she was dealing with it.

My immediate reaction was one of total surprise and sadness. Thinking that this might be the end, I said, "Can I still pop over and see you when I come up?"

"Of course," she said. "That would be very nice."

It was time to go. I stood up and moved to give Carla a hug, which led to a kiss, and another hug goodnight.

Across the garden we waved to each other and pulled our respective curtains.

Carla made the most of her time, and seemed to enjoy our get-together despite our age difference, which did not seem to matter at all.

The last time we met I did realise my initial fantasy, and saw Carla in full view (which I was unable to see across the garden). I arrived early to pick her up and she ran downstairs to answer the door in her underwear. I was not disappointed. Over our next meal she asked me if at the appropriate time I would make contact with her family, who lived in Surrey. She had had a fall-out with them some years ago and wanted to make them aware of her fate.

Six months or so later Carla passed away. She had given me all the details to be able to make the necessary calls to her family, etc., and she had left information about her funeral wishes. Of course calling her family was not easy, but I explained that due to her illness she had to work reduced hours as a solicitor. I think they took on board my comments, although I was only one of a handful of people who attended the funeral service.

Walking away from the church after the service, I was delighted to have been seduced by such a brave women, even though it was for such a short period of time.

TWO WIVES UNDER ONE ROOF

Autumn was beginning to show its true colours, which usually made a delightful scene. Golden leaves falling from the trees, and occasional warm sunshine with a little nip in the air to tell us, 'Forget summer; winter is on its way.'

Doris, Joan and Harry were all residents in the Elders Care Home, across the road from the seafront in Milton-by-the-Sea – a seafront which in the summer months bustled with people on holiday. Milton was a very pleasant place to live. The care home was ideally located with most residents having a sea view to wake up to. Some called it magical.

Doris was eighty-four. She was fit and healthy; Joan, who had a birthday due in a week's time, would be eighty-seven; and dear old Harry topped them all at the age of eighty-nine. Ellie was the manager of the Elders. She looked after them all and made sure that whatever the residents did they enjoyed it, and had fun.

It was a cold November morning. The sun was shining brightly and breakfast was well under way. As he finished his toast and marmalade, Harry thought a walk along the seafront would be good.

"Are you two girls going to join me for a stroll along the seafront this morning?" he asked.

Doris nodded as she ate her porridge; however, Joan did not appear enthusiastic as she finished her boiled egg.

"I am going back to my room to have a lie-down," she said.

"You've only just got up!" exclaimed Harry

Doris gave him a gentle kick under the table. "Let her be," she said.

Thirty minutes later, and with coats, scarves and hats at the ready, Harry and Doris carefully crossed the road and started their stroll along the seafront. Their walk usually lasted for an hour, and included a coffee stop. On the way back they popped into the beach café and enjoyed a coffee – after all, it was such a lovely day. They talked for a while about family and friends and the number of people still around seemingly on holiday. Soon the conversation came around to Joan.

"She seems to have been a bit off colour over the past few days," said Doris.

"Well, it would have done her some good to come out with us this morning," added Harry.

"You don't think she suspects anything, do you?" Doris asked.

"Well, I have not said a word. Anyway, put like that you make it all sound very unsavoury," Harry added.

Having walked a few hundred yards further on, Harry stopped again and sat down on a bench which looked out to sea. Doris was more than a little concerned as she joined him.

"Are you OK?" she asked.

"Why do you ask?" Harry replied.

"Well, you don't appear to be yourself," said Doris.

"Bloody indigestion, I think," Harry offered.

"Are you sure?" Doris challenged.

"I think so," Harry simply replied.

After a few minutes they rose from the bench and strolled back to the Elders, where the smell of lunch was emanating from the kitchen.

Following their lunch they all went to either the lounge or their rooms for a snooze. However, Joan heard a commotion downstairs and wondered what was going on. She decided to take a look. As she arrived downstairs she could see the flashing lights of an ambulance, and a worried-looking Ellie.

"Who is that going out in a stretcher and into the ambulance?" Joan asked.

"Harry," Ellie said. "He is not feeling too well. The

paramedic came and thought he should go to hospital and get checked out," she continued.

"Is anyone with him?" Joan asked.

"Oh yes, Doris is going with him," Ellie said.

"Why Doris?" Joan continued.

"Well, she is his wife," Ellie confirmed.

With that, Joan went a very pale colour, and Ellie, realising this, guided her to a seat nearby.

"Why are you upset, Joan?" Ellie asked.

"Well, Harry was my first husband, and we discussed coming here and living independently, but he has never told me that he had got married again. I don't mind, but it is a bit of a shock."

The following morning Joan had breakfast on her own and wondered when she would hear news about Harry. She had been back in her room for approximately an hour when there was a knock on the door. Opening the door, she saw Harry and a smile came to her face.

"How are you?" she asked.

"Better now," Harry announced.

"I am pleased to see you," Joan added.

"Enough about me – I owe you an apology," Harry added. "In fact, a belated apology," he continued.

Before Joan could say another word Harry had given her chapter and verse on how he had met Doris, and how they had fallen for each other, and then married. Then, as both had had illnesses they made a decision to sell their bungalow and come to the Elders and live out their time there in comfort.

"Harry, there is no need to explain. Ellie told me, and that is fine with me," she confirmed.

As Doris and Harry enjoyed a sherry before their lunch, Joan arrived with a broad smile on her face.

"I have some news," she said.

"Oh?" said Harry.

"I have had a call from Sue and David. They want to pop in a see us tomorrow and they are bringing Annabelle with them," she enthused.

"Well, that will be a pleasure," added Harry.

Joan added that she had spoken to Ellie and arranged for them to have a cream tea in the library.

"How old is Annabelle now?" asked Harry.

"Oh, I think early twenties."

The following afternoon at approximately 2 p.m. the doorbell rang. Ellie answered it and greeted Sue, David and Annabelle.

"Do come in," she said. "I'll show you to the library, where we have afternoon tea laid on for you."

A few minutes later Joan arrived and was having hugs and kisses when Harry came into the room.

"Hello. How are you all?" he asked.

"We are fine – very pleased to see you both looking so good," enthused Sue.

With that, the door opened again and in walked Doris.

Sue and David looked at her as if to say, "Who are you?"

Harry put his arm around Doris and introduced her to everyone: "Doris is my wife," Harry said.

"Wha-a-a-a-a-a-at?" asked Sue. "Mum, what is going on?"

Joan asked everyone to sit whilst she explained.

After about ten minutes Joan thought she had explained everything clearly, but Harry stood up and said, "Actually, that is not all. It is quite possible that after what I am now going to tell you all you might want to call the police and have me arrested."

"What on earth are you talking about?" implored Doris and Joan.

"Well," – looking at Joan, Harry continued – "when we agreed to get divorced I brought all the necessary papers around for you to sign."

"Yes, and I signed them," Joan said.

"I agree, but . . . Oh Lord – I really didn't want to lose you, but I wanted Doris as well, so I thought about it a long time, and I didn't sign them."

Doris's face was white with shock. "You mean you are still married to both of us?"

Coyly Harry said, "Well, yes, I suppose, I am."

Uproar followed, and Joan and Doris comforted each other, shocked by the news they had just heard.

In the midst of the chaos, Ellie thought it was time to call in to see when they wanted tea to be served. She did not expect to find such anguish and upset, so backed out of the room quickly.

'Perhaps I will leave it another thirty minutes,' she thought to herself.

With David talking to Harry, and Sue consoling her mum and Doris, Annabelle wondered why she had decided to come at all.

"Excuse me," she shouted.

Everyone looked up.

"Can I say something?" she asked.

Everyone nodded.

"OK. This is a tricky situation indeed; however, clearly we have a choice to make. Or should I say that the three oldies have a choice? One option is the police are called, and they do what they have to, and resolve the matter through the courts, or . . ." And turning towards Joan she asked, "Do you still love Harry?"

"Yes, I suppose I do," said Joan.

"Doris, do you still love this man you married, even though he appears to be a dirty cheat?" she asked.

"It seems strange put that way; but yes, I think I do," Doris admitted.

"So", continued Annabelle, "why [looking at her grandma] is it necessary for us to get involved at all? After all, they live here together now and nobody need know. Why not let things go on as they are now!"

Somewhat relieved, Harry said, "What a sensible thought!"

"You be quiet! It is you, remember, that has caused this headache," Joan said firmly.

Ellie found enough courage to knock on the library door, and asked if they wanted tea.

The firm reply was "Yes, please, or have you anything stronger?"

The refreshments were brought in, and very gradually Annabelle's comments were accepted as the way forward.

"We must all be very tight-lipped and carry on as before. And you [looking at Harry] start treating these lovely ladies – or should I say your two wives? – with more respect," she said.

"I humbly apologise," Harry said.

At 5.30 p.m. Sue, David and Annabelle left the Elders, and Harry and his two wives settled into a more open and honest relationship.

BABIES IN THE WOODS

St Mark's Parish Church was full for the Sunday service. This was not always the case. Congregations across the religious divide seemed to be falling – but not today apparently.

As I sat towards the back of the church I cast an eye over those in front, and scanned those who were locals and those who were visitors. The latter no doubt were spending the weekend with family or friends. Some of the locals I knew as regular churchgoers, and generally they were a nice crowd.

The hymn finished and next came the sermon – not always the highlight of the Sunday-morning service. It either sends you to sleep or makes you sit up and listen. First were the notices – a summary of next week's events and news from around the parish. Then came the banns of marriage. With bated breath we waited to hear what would follow.

Lena Dearing from the parish of St Peter the Redeemer, some twenty miles away, was to marry Mike Sampson of this parish, and this, the vicar added, was after the third time of asking. This always makes me smile. After all, I asked Sue to marry me once, and she said yes, so why would anyone have to ask three times?

The sermon was today thankfully short, allowing the service to be completed in an hour. As the congregation filed out through the seventeenth-century vestibule into the bright sunshine, various groups gathered for a chat – mostly, I guess, about Annie Jones's flamboyant hat! It never ceases to amaze me that, having just come out of church, people seize upon a trivial point like a hat, or suchlike.

"Hello, Mary," I said, seeing Mary and George Bennett. "How are you both?"

They smiled back and said they were fine.

Edith and Dan Marks were also close by, and we entered into a brief chat about this and that.

"Do you know this Mike Sampson?" I asked.

"No. He's new to the area, I believe," said Dan.

So jokingly I added, "Are you going to the wedding, then?"

He smiled and said he wasn't.

Edith then added, "It's a lovely church to be married in. Anyway, we must be going. We have a table booked for lunch at the Green Lantern."

"Enjoy!" I added.

I slowly drove home with a strangely cheeky idea in my head, all about going to a wedding as an uninvited guest. Sue and I had chatted about it sometime ago, but we never really developed the thought further.

When I arrived home I could see that Sue was home from her tennis lesson. She was about to pour herself a glass of Pinot Grigio as I came through the door.

"How was church?" she asked.

"Oh, fine. The usual suspects were there. Could you pour me a glass too, and I will quickly change," I added.

A few minutes later we were relaxing under the gazebo in the garden, sipping our cold wine.

"Ever heard of a Mike Sampson?" I asked.

"No – why?" Sue replied.

"He is going to marry a Lena Dearing from the Barton area. Their banns were read out in church today. Since then I have had a cheeky thought about uninvited guests going to weddings," I continued. "We did chat about it sometime ago. Do you remember?"

"Yes, I do. So you fancy having some fun, do you?" Sue asked.

"Why not?" I said.

"OK, let's plan it out and consider a few things and look at the calendar and we will try it. Who knows – we might make a habit of it!" suggested Sue.

We finished our glass of Pinot, locked up and strolled to the Red Plucker pub, just off the High Street, where we had booked a table for a 2 p.m. lunch. Brian, the landlord, greeted us, and pointed to table 17 in the corner. We settled at the table and considered the menu. I then asked Sue what she would like to drink, and she said another glass of Pinot. At the bar I ordered Sue's drink and a pint of Peroni, which Brian said he would bring over. We ordered our lunch and sipped our drinks. Due to the intimate nature of the restaurant, some conversations could be overheard, and sure enough this made interesting listening. It seemed like a preview for the very wedding we were contemplating going to. By the time we heard that there was to be a marquee, a buffet and live music, Sue and I had confirmed to each other that we would very much like to go.

Two Weeks Later

It was yet another warm and sunny day and we were looking forward to the day ahead. We drove to Barton, finding the church easily. Close by was the marquee, within easy walking distance of the church. We seemed to have timed things about right. The bride had just gone through the church doors, and we eased into the back seats unnoticed.

The service was all over after about forty-five minutes. This was followed by the photos, for which Sue and I became invisible.

"Lovely service,' a voice said.

"Yes, it was," Sue and I chorused.

Thankfully that conversation did not develop.

The guests then dispersed, strolling towards the marquee and the bar, and of course the reception. Thankfully it was a really warm day; otherwise most of the ladies would I am sure have ended up with a cold judging by the way they dressed with so little on. Short skirts – in fact, some *very* short skirts – were plentiful, as were very low tops struggling to keep some big chests in place and loads of make-up. Not nice! Drinks seemed to flow liberally in that first hour or so, and some guests were already looking worse for wear.

The buffet was wonderful, and once again we did engage in a brief chat whilst queuing, plate in hand, for the salad.

"Have you travelled far?" we were asked.

"Not really" was our brief reply.

"Are you bride or groom?" was the next question – one which we managed to fend off.

Then a voice said, "Hi, John. Didn't expect to see you here."

I turned and the voice apologised – he thought I was someone else. Phew!

We took our food and were refilling our glasses when someone said, "Are you enjoying yourselves?"

"Very much," I replied as I turned to see who was asking.

"I'm Trevor. And you are?" he asked.

"Oh, my wife and I are old friends of [choosing now to opt for the bride] Lena's."

"Ah, I thought you might be. I'm the best man."

I just added, "Lovely day."

He nodded and moved back to the main crowd.

I looked around for Sue and found her being chatted up by a younger man – wanting to walk her to the woods, I guess.

'Fat chance!' I thought triumphantly.

We made our way to a raised area, away from the masses, where we could see all the goings-on. There was lots of flirting, and bridesmaids were seemingly well prepared for approaches by ushers.

We were now several hours into this wedding, which, to be fair, was very well organised. Good job it wasn't ticket-only! Tipsy young ladies were now being snogged by young guys thinking that their luck might be about to change. For some Sue and I thought it would, as we could clearly see from our vantage point couples drifting off into the woods with a half-bottle of wine.

"Why do people – especially young ladies, it seems – have tattoos?" I questioned Sue.

"I'm not really sure," she said.

As I heard her reply, I pointed to a disappearing couple. The woman had both arms heavily tattooed.

Sue shook her head.

The live music started up, and as daylight became night the atmosphere changed to a more intimate setting. Sue and I decided to slip away and make our way home. All in all we had enjoyed our day. It was a lovely wedding service, with a good substantial buffet, some fabulous weather and plenty of seduction on view. We had come through the experience unscathed, and after a glass of Scotch we climbed the stairs to our bed.

Nine Months Later

Sue had called to say she was going to be late home due to a couple of patients being added to her clinic list. However, when she did come through the door she looked shocked and eager to tell a story.

I could tell something was up, so I said, "OK, what is it?"

"Firstly, let me change and I will reveal all when I come down."

Sue emerged from upstairs, and with the air of a newscaster about to announce a major story she started.

"Do you recall the wedding in Barton?" she asked.

"Yes, I do. Why?"

"Do you remember the girl – the attractive blonde with the tattooed arms – slipping off into the woods with a young man?"

"Yes, I do. Why?"

"Well, she came into the clinic this afternoon with her baby."

"What!" I exclaimed.

"After a few questions it became clear that those woods are Trouble, with a capital T, if you're not careful – and it appears she was not careful." Sue continued: "And the father is not only many years older than her, but he's married."

"Oh, my God, what a mess!" I said.

Eighteen Months Later

We now had been to several weddings as uninvited guests. It was fun, and luckily we were never caught out. The idea of attending another one was rather exciting, so when Sue read in the local paper that there was to be a wedding in two weeks' time we became rather excited and decided to go once again to Barton. We arrived again just in time, and sat at the back as before. After the service we again avoided getting involved with photos, and proceeded to the tented area and to the waitresses with trays of champagne. Seizing two glasses, we quickly moved away from the main wedding party. There was a barbecue close by which was smelling lovely, and it did not take long to join the others queuing for steak and sausages, etc.

As time progressed we needed to stretch our legs, so with refilled glasses we made our way towards the woods to view this Trouble (with a capital T) area.

On our return, a disco had started. It was far too loud, which was a shame and it seemed to spoil the whole event. Thirty minutes later we decided to make a move and we slipped away, home.

Two Months Later

As I poured a G & T, Sue, who had just come through the door, said "Just a small one for me, please."

"Oh, why?" I enquired.

"The woods at Barton" was all she said, adding, "They are quite magical really!"

"What are you talking about?" I asked.

"The walk we had through them and . . . you know what I mean," she continued.

"Yes," I added. I thought for a moment or two, and then the penny dropped. "You mean . . . ?" I asked.

"Yes, I think I'm pregnant. Isn't that wonderful news!" she enthused.

We sat down with our drinks to absorb the news that in a

few months' time we would be a family of three. Sam would be with us, and that would end our exploits of gate-crashing weddings and our lives would change forever.

"I must call my sister and give her the news. She will be over the moon," I said.

"Eve will be thrilled," added Sue. "In fact why don't we arrange to go down to Wellington and see her?" she continued.

"I will call her later," I said.

Later That Evening

Ring, ring-ring, ring.

"Hello. Eve, it's David. How are you?"

"Hi, Dave. Good to hear from you. Yeah, we're fine, thank you. And Sue?"

"All good," I added. "Hang on – what is this *we*?" I enquired.

"Ah, Geoff and I met at Grandad's funeral, which you and Sue could not come to as you were away on holiday."

"OK. Well, perhaps we could meet him when we come down?"

"I would love that. When can you come down?" she asked,

"How about at the weekend?" I cheekily asked. "Only we have something to tell you, and I am not going to go into details over the phone," I said.

"Sounds exciting! Can I guess? No, I won't, but I'll see you Friday evening for supper, then," she confirmed.

"Lovely. See you then."

Friday Evening

"Dave, Sue, this is Geoff, my man," Eve introduced us excitedly.

"Delighted to meet you," Sue and I chorused.

As we sat down to our supper Eve was clearly keen to hear our news, which we could not hold on to for very long.

"I am pregnant," said Sue with a gleaming smile.

All Eve could say was "I knew it, I knew it."

We then told them the story of our wedding exploits, and we all had a great laugh.

"Anyway, how about you two? Tell us more – how you met, etc., etc.," said Sue.

With that they both burst out laughing, and told us what they had been doing.

"Funerals? Really? Like brother, like sister, I guess," I added.

With that Geoff appeared with four glasses and a bottle of Prosecco to celebrate our news.

WHO'S BEEN SLEEPING IN MY BED?

The new resort was situated on the west coast of the Canary Island of Fuerteventura. It was built with the idea of attracting buyers from across Europe, for whom an early retirement home or a holiday hideaway could be made into a distinct possibility.

Simon and Petra led very stressful lives. Simon was a solicitor and Petra a housing manager with the council in West Sussex. Both were looking ahead and planning their retirements, which they hoped would be possible within the next four years.

Going through the weekend papers, they came across an advert promoting two- and three-bedroom apartments in the Canarian resort. Could this fit their plans? After a lengthy chat they decided to obtain a brochure and the all-important price list.

Towards the end of the following week the brochures arrived, and to their amazement what they read and saw heightened their sense of excitement about having their own place in the sun. The prices seemed reasonable. An apartment was something they could afford, so they agreed to chat about it further over breakfast the following morning.

Well, all that was some ten months or so ago and now the day came to fly out to Fuerteventura and pick up the keys to their apartment. Yes, it would be a place which would be used initially on a part-time basis, but when they retired it would really come into its own.

The four-hour flight was on time, and as they walked from the plane towards passport control they could feel the warmth that the island exudes. Simon and Petra floated through baggage handling towards the car-hire office, knowing they were only a short drive away from their holiday home.

Within an hour of landing, collecting their hire car and signing for the apartment keys, they excitedly opened the door of their new home and cracked open a bottle of cava to celebrate. The next few days were to be spent enjoying their new surroundings and exploring the area.

Many years now passed, and Simon and Petra retired and were spending more and more time on Fuerteventura. They were thrilled with their investment and enjoying their second home, which had materially changed from the original apartment they first moved into. They had new patio furniture, a new settee, a smart TV and a super new cooker.

In the UK Simon was a keen golfer, and when contemplating moving to the Canary Islands he made the decision to join the Sallinas Club in Caleta de Fuste. This enabled him to meet new people and develop new friendships. Petra became more and more involved with the local community, and soon became friendly with a few people with similar interests.

After an exhausting eighteen holes one day, Simon got chatting to Dean, and soon discovered they were neighbours. In fact they lived only three apartments away from each other.

"You must come around for a drink," said Simon, "and bring your wife, of course."

"That would be nice," said Dean. "How about tomorrow afternoon?"

They agreed and went home.

Arriving back at the apartment, Simon was keen to tell Petra all about his new golfing buddy, and how he had invited Dean and his wife around for a drink the following afternoon.

"Lovely," said Petra.

The door buzzer buzzed and Dean introduced his wife, Mary, to Simon and Petra. Simon likewise introduced Petra. Conversation naturally centred on where in the UK they came from and how long they had had their apartments. Over a few glasses of wine they soon discovered that they had a lot in common. They decided to have a meal out together sometime, to broaden the conversation somewhat.

"Tell me," said Petra: "who looks after your apartment when you go back to the UK?"

"Oh," said Mary, "we live here all the time. Our respective parents died some years ago and we have no family, so here we are, residents. Why?"

"Ah, I was just wondering who could keep an eye on ours whilst we are away. In a couple of weeks we have to go back for a month to sort out a few things," said Petra.

"Well, I expect we could. We keep an eye on a few others," said Mary.

"That would be reassuring," said Petra.

Unknown to Simon and Petra, and to the other apartment owners who were looked after by Dean and Mary, their homes were not only kept an eye on, but they were occasionally lived in whilst their owners were away. They took advantage of being keyholders and decided whose apartment they would use next.

Some days had passed since Simon and Petra had gone back to the UK and Dean decided to pop into Simon and Petra's home. The electricity and water were still on, and food and drinks were in the fridge.

"It looks ready for a weekend visit," said Dean.

So he and Mary decided when they would move in for a two-night stay.

"We are at Belle and John's next, then Tricia and Martin's, so after that sounds good," said Mary.

The weekend came, and after a beer or two they studied the fridge with a meal in mind.

"Do you think they will miss that steak?" asked Mary.

"Not a chance," said Dean.

They enjoyed watching the new smart TV and eating someone else's food.

Back in the UK Simon and Petra managed to deal with all their business earlier than they had first thought, and they booked flights back out to Fuerteventura earlier than planned.

'How lovely to be going back to the sun and our new-found friends!' they thought.

The flight was later than they had hoped for, leaving the UK at 6 p.m. and arriving at approximately 10.30 p.m.

The flight went to plan, but in the following hours that would be all that did. On arrival they picked up the hire car and drove to their apartment.

Dean and Mary decided to have an early night, finding their afternoon siesta in Simon and Petra's bed very comfortable indeed. Undressed and ready for bed, they suddenly heard the door unlock and – shock horror! – both couples stood momentarily speechless. Split seconds later, raised voices could be heard. Hurriedly Dean and Mary grabbed their clothes and left.

"I thought they were our friends," said Petra.

Belle and John from next door heard the commotion and went to see if all was OK."

"Most certainly not," said Simon, and he outlined what had happened.

Belle, who seemed deep in thought for a moment or two, then turned to John and said, "Do you know, when we have come back, having been away for a couple of weeks, I often wonder who's been sleeping in my bed? Sounds silly, I know, but I think I now know who it is."

SO FAR BUT YET SO NEAR

The florist shop in the Market Square which was linked with the funeral business of Dyer & Bury was so popular with the local community. It was not occasionally busy, but very busy all the time. Harriet and Abi worked very hard to keep customers happy, and were thrilled to receive their first order for wedding flowers. The wedding was to be in three weeks' time.

"Well, if they have weather like we are currently having, it will be fantastic," said Abi.

"I have never been to St Joseph's before, have you?" asked Harriet.

"Once, I think," Abi admitted. "My christening," she continued, laughing.

"Well, as it will be our very first wedding, perhaps we ought to go and admire our handiwork," Abi suggested.

"That is an excellent idea," said Harriet eagerly.

The current spell of hot weather was having an exhausting effect on everyone, and as the shop did not have air conditioning it was very stuffy indeed. So the door and windows were opened to allow a flow of air to filter through.

Two Weeks Later

"Phew, it is hot again today," said Harriet.

With that the phone rang, and the call resulted in two orders for funeral flowers. They were for large funerals too – one was of a gentleman, Mr Dyson, aged eighty-two, and the other was of a Mr Hardaker, aged eighty-seven. They were both local gentlemen and their funerals would attract large congregations. The dates for these two funerals were confirmed as the Thursday before the wedding, which was a work in progress. The shop's workload was increasing, with more wedding enquiries and, sadly, more funerals.

"I don't know about you," said Abi, "but I think I am going to work overnight on Wednesday. It will be cooler to prepare the wreaths for Thursday's funeral and the other flower orders we have in," she continued.

"Oh, that is a good idea," said Harriet. "If you like I will come in early on Thursday morning to help finish off," she added.

"That will be a great help," Abi said.

At 5.30 p.m. the shop closed. The blinds came down and the doors were locked. Harriet went home and Abi continued in the cooling heat. After a couple of hours or so Abi was feeling a tad peckish, and she decided to go and get a pizza. Whilst in the queue she bumped into an old friend she had not seen for a very long time.

"Susie, how the hell are you?" Abi yelled. "I haven't seen you since . . . when?"

"My mother's birthday back in March. She was fifty, do you remember?" Susie interjected.

"Yes, I do recall. How is she?" Abi asked.

"Well, actually, very well," Susie said. "Come and have a drink with me," Susie pleaded.

"Well, that is going to be difficult," Abi said. "We are so busy that I am working through the night to prepare for two funerals in the morning," Abi explained.

"Oh, come on – one drink," Susie suggested.

"Oh, OK then," said Abi, weakening.

So off to the Sippers Wine Bar they went.

The Sippers Wine Bar, situated across the square, was not too busy; however, two glasses of Shiraz later Abi was feeling quite tired and could not stop yawning.

"Look," she said, "as much as I have really enjoyed this brief catch-up, and would like very much to stay longer, work beckons. So I must go," she added.

"Please give me a call – say, next week?" Abi suggested.

Susie said goodbye and said she would call her.

Abi headed back to work and entered the shop via the back door, locking it behind her. As she continued to prepare the flowers, Abi felt she needed to check the names and other details of the two funerals for the following morning; so she took the keys and went to the chapel of rest, where all the paperwork lay on the floor next to each coffin. The first thing she noticed was how cool it was.

'Lovely!' she thought.

Here the two bodies were lying in their coffins ready to be collected by the bearers in the morning.

After checking a couple of things, she muttered to herself, "Ah, that is Mr Dyson and that is Mr Hardaker."

There were other coffins on the floor ready for future funerals, and something drew Abi to have a closer look at them. Abi was yawning and feeling very drowsy. She thought, 'I really ought to be in my bed.' After another series of yawns Abi had another thought: 'If I could just have forty winks, I would feel much better,' she said to herself. Glancing at the open coffin nearest her, she thought how comfortable it appeared, all padded out, and she wondered what it felt like to lie inside one. This of course was not an important factor for the person who, sadly, would lie in it, but she thought it would be interesting to slip into one anyhow to check it out.

Abi eased herself into the coffin and thought it was very comfortable – too comfortable actually, as seemingly within seconds Abi was fast asleep. After an hour or so Abi stretched and turned in her sleep, as if she was in her bed at home. With that the lid closed, but her sleep continued.

It was eight thirty the following morning when, as promised, Harriet arrived, earlier than normal. She found the shop lights on, but no Abi. Thinking that Abi must have gone home to sleep at some stage, she proceeded to finish off the flowers which Abi had started arranging the night before. Whilst she was finishing off the last spray, the hearse came into the yard and the bearers opened up the chapel of rest to pick up the first coffin for the first funeral of the day. The bearers picked up the paperwork alongside the coffin on the floor and then slid the coffin, thought to contain Mr Dyson, into the hearse. After closing the doors, they then eased out into the traffic and slowly drove towards St David's Church, ten miles away.

The morning traffic was building up and progress was rather slow. However as they approached the second set of traffic lights five minutes into the trip the driver and pallbearers heard a distinct knocking sound.

Bob said, "I thought that bearing was sorted during the service last week."

Tom nodded in agreement as they proceeded to the next set of lights.

More knocking followed, so Bob decided to pull into a lay-by and investigate. As the hearse came to a stop, the lid of the coffin flew open and Abi's head appeared. Everyone at this point started to get out of the vehicle in fright.

"What on earth are you doing?" asked Bob.

Abi explained and at that moment another funeral car came up behind them. To save embarrassment Bob said that they had a small problem and had to return to the yard, but would only be a few minutes late. Needless to say, they then sped back to the yard, where Abi slipped out of her comfortable coffin. Mr Dyson was loaded into the hearse and taken successfully to St David's for a funeral service followed by a burial.

Looking at Abi, Harriet seemed speechless, but she just had to ask, "What on earth were you doing?"

Before Abi could answer, the two burst into laughter.

"You do realise you were well on your way to meet your Maker much earlier than planned," Harriet explained.

"That's not funny," said Abi.

When she had outlined her story completely, more laughter could be heard down the High Street.

"Cadging a lift is one thing," said Harriet, "but stowing away in a hearse is a bit desperate, don't you think?"

"Very funny," said Abi. "Now let us think about the wedding flowers."

LIFE IN THE MASSAGE PARLOUR

It was Friday afternoon. Virtually all the production for the week had been completed and a mass tidy-up was under way. However, left over in three buckets was some modelling clay, and I had decided to make one or two oddments rather than dump it into a waste skip.

I found an old mould on a shelf above me – a mould for a Buddha about eight to nine inches high – and I was eager to give it a go. I made twelve in all, and I must say they did look quite good – very Buddha-like.

Classic Chinaware UK was based near Stoke-on-Trent, in the Midlands, and its main business was producing quality pottery, with the majority of the products being exported. We were always busy, but this weekend we were closed for maintenance, so that would allow the day's production, plus a dozen Buddhas, to cure before Monday.

Monday morning came soon enough, and firstly we all started to move Friday's production on to the next stage. Mid morning my internal phone rang.

"Hello," I said.

"Ed, what on earth have you sent me?" the voice asked.

I chuckled. "Are you referring to my Buddhas?" I asked.

"Oh, is that what they are?" I was asked.

"Look – just do your best to rough off the edges and spray them a dark grey, please,' I suggested.

Twenty-four hours later a couple of boxes came back to me with the model Buddhas enclosed. I excitedly opened the first box and picked one up to see if my little experiment had been a success. I smiled. 'This might become a new line,' I thought. 'No way!' But it was fun to see how they turned out.

Some weeks earlier I had spoken to a friend of mine, Cliff Stoneman, who owned a shop which sold novelty items such as the ones I had just made. So I called him and arranged for him to come over and take a look. On Wednesday morning Cliff visited the works, and he seemed very pleased with the little men we had made.

"I'll take them," he said.

So we loaded them into his van, and I wished him good luck selling them. Unknown to me at this time was that the minute the Buddhas left us they became alive!

My name is Abdul and this is my story. A new day had started and we were on a journey – a journey to where? No doubt we would soon find out. Bright lights then appeared and our boxes were opened. We were then picked up and placed on a stand for people to see.

A label was then attached to us, and Olly, one of the Buddhas, said, "What does that label say?"

Stretching a little, I said, "It says you are £20."

Indignantly Olly said, "That's not a lot – I think we are worth more than that."

Days and days went by and we lost count of the number of times we were picked up and put down again. I decided that it was time to have a little fun to ease the boredom, so I suggested to Olly that when the next people picked us up we should poke our tongues out at them.

Olly sniggered. "I can't wait to see their reaction to that," he added.

Shoppers were not too plentiful, but a lady and two young children appeared in front of us.

"Look, Mummy, look," said one of the children as they picked me up.

I poked my tongue out, and a scream followed. I was lucky not to find myself in pieces.

"Put it down!" was the mother's plea, and I was duly placed safely back on the shelf.

"It poked its tongue out – it really did," said the child.

"Yes, dear," said her mum, and they moved on.

The other child thought he would look more closely at Olly, so he carefully picked him up, at which point Olly winked. He nearly crashed to the floor like me, but made it back to the shelf unscathed. Off the little boy went, yelling to his mum, who paid little attention to her children's suggestions.

That was our fun for the day. We did play the same tricks on others, which caused us to have a giggle, but nothing more than that.

Three months later we were still there.

"I'm not sure about you," said Olly, "but I would very much like to get out of here."

"I was only thinking the same thing yesterday. It would be exciting to have a new adventure," I added.

"I mean, there are only so many times you can poke your tongue out at people, or wink." Olly sadly offered.

With that an early couple of shoppers approached our shelf, and a steady pair of hands picked us up. Without too much consideration we were placed carefully in a basket, and we thought we were being taken for a walk around the shop. To our pleasant surprise we did not end up back on our shelf; we were placed back in the boxes we came in and slipped into a bag.

A muffled voice said, "Where are we going?" It was Olly.

"You wanted to get out of here, so let's wait and see," I suggested.

Sometime later we were taken out of the box and placed on a new shelf, and a voice said, "Oh, they are ideal."

'Ideal for what?' I wondered. Then we were back in the box again, and we wondered what would happen next.

Later that day we found ourselves in a bigger bag, and I heard voices talking about a trip by aeroplane (whatever that is) to a new home in the sun. Well, that did not bother us – we were used to hot weather, so interesting times were ahead, it seemed.

A few days later we once again were picked out of our box, only this time we were placed on a table in the corner of a smallish room, with bright sunshine pouring through the window. In the middle of the room was a bed-type thing with coloured towels on it. This all appeared rather strange, but all would be revealed in due course, I guessed.

"Where on earth are we?" Olly quietly asked.

"Sh-h-h!" was all I could muster.

I decided, with all the recent activity, I would have a rest. Olly, I think, soon followed.

Morning came, and I heard voices getting nearer to our room. The door opened and in walked two people. One was a lady called Gerda (strange name, I thought – nearly as strange as mine) and the other was a lady called Susie. After a few words the lady went behind a screen to wash her hands, and Susie started taking her clothes off!

"Olly, don't look! Close your eyes – both of them!" I suggested.

"What about you?" asked Olly.

"I will tell you all about it later," I offered.

"Hell to that!" Olly said. "If you are going to watch, so am I," he eagerly said.

Gerda then reappeared and, with Susie face down on the bed, started to gently guide her hands over Susie's back.

"Hey, what's her game?" asked Olly, not content with just watching.

After about an hour, with Susie turning over at one point, it was all over. All we could hear was Susie saying it was a great massage.

'Is that what they call it?' I thought.

"Oh, my God!" shouted Olly.

"Oh, that's good coming from a Buddha," I countered.

"Well, you know what I mean – I didn't expect that, did you?"

"No, I didn't, but it was all very gentle and very peaceful. I wonder when the next one will come?" I queried.

It did not take long before the door opened again, and this time a man appeared. The same thing happened as before, but this man, called George, was big and could certainly lose a few pounds.

"Is he a real Buddha?" asked Olly.

"Don't be daft," I told him.

As George lay on his front, once again Gerda worked her magic. Olly, who was becoming less shy, did though close one eye when George turned over.

"I think", he whispered, "that's not a pretty sight," but then Olly would say that.

Olly and I spent many years with Gerda in her room in the sun. We saw many people of various shapes and sizes and had fun talking about them. Then one day Olly was no longer on the corner of the table – he was being cleaned, and sadly he was dropped. He smashed into many pieces. So now I am alone and have no one to chat to.

This story is dedicated to Jenny R., who always thought 'The Art of Disguise and Deception 1' could develop into another story. So here it is, Jen. And thank you for all your kind words and encouragement.

THE ART OF DISGUISE AND DECEPTION 1

The Greek island of Skiathos was our chosen place; mind you, it could so easily have been Kos, Corfu or Rhodes for our holiday in the sun, with golden sand and a warm sea to bathe in. Ah, Greece – simply Greece! Two weeks' relaxation, where we could forget any troubles that we had, and recharge the batteries!

As usual the M42 was busy and the traffic heavy. There always seemed to be someone going somewhere, lanes full with every vehicle one could imagine. I was delighted to see the sign for junction 6, the turn-off for the NEC and Birmingham International Airport. Now we had to locate our hotel and park. Our departure times were early the following morning, so we decided to stay overnight and get to the terminal early the next day. The hotel was easy to find, as was a parking space, and we booked in at reception. After a quick shower we found the restaurant for a meal and a much needed drink. Sofia, my Colombian girlfriend, ordered a large glass of Pinot Grigio and I had a large Rioja. Relaxing, we viewed the menu, decided what to order and chatted about the two weeks ahead.

In a split second I had a flashback to when Sofia and I first met. It was in Holland on one of those city breaks – a four-day job for £110 all-inclusive. Amsterdam is such a vibrant city and of course almost anything can happen at any time. I suppose a summary of Amsterdam would be 'Sex, drugs and rock and roll', but that might be a tad unfair. The queue for the canal boat was quite long, and I thought at first I would not get on. In fact I did, with this attractive lady, taking the last couple of seats. It was a relaxing couple of hours, though we cringed at some of the low bridges, debating whether we would fit underneath.

At the end of the trip the boat docked and Sofia (I did not know her name at this point) and I were first off. As we gathered our thoughts I boldly asked the lady if she fancied a coffee, and she nodded yes. That was the start of it really. Some two hours or so later we were having a meal together. I walked her back to her hotel, now Chris and Sofia, and we agreed to meet in the morning.

"Hello-o-o-o, Chris. Are you OK?"
"Pardon? Oh yes, sorry – I drifted off."
"Anywhere interesting?" she asked.
"To Amsterdam, where we first met," I told her.
"Lovely memories," she added as our meals arrived.

Sofia and I had been together now for three years or so. After coming back from Amsterdam we kept in contact, and it wasn't long before we moved in together. She was a lot younger than I, but she was something special, with a gorgeous figure, and she was fun to be with. She always caused a stir when we went to our local, and many of my friends asked me if she had a sister! The answer was in fact she had two brothers and a sister all a lot younger than her. I felt very lucky to have a twenty-five-year-old as my girlfriend. Sofia spoke sufficient English to get by, and when she got it wrong it always created a laugh or two. She had moved here from Bogotá five years ago to study travel, banking and financial planning at Nottingham University. This was the end of her studies, so this trip was a sort of celebration of her course finishing.

After a passionate night in our king-size bed, we managed to be up in time to catch the courtesy bus to the airport. Booking in our bags, we made our way through passport control, then through security, before finding a seat in the departure lounge. Excited at just being there, we had independent strolls around the area, keeping an eye on gate numbers, etc., so we wouldn't miss our departure. As Sofia was looking around I noticed that our gate number had flashed up, so I tried to attract her attention. When she saw me, she nodded and intimated she would go to the toilet before we walked to gate 22, and our flight to Skiathos.

We were forty-five minutes away from take-off, and it was approximately a fifteen-minute walk to gate 22, so I was getting more than a little concerned about the time Sofia was taking in the Ladies. Ten minutes later I was becoming very anxious – so much so that I made my way towards the toilets. It was busy, but still no Sofia appeared. I decided to ask another lady passenger if she could take a look for me, but that proved no use. Where the hell had she gone?

I ran to gate 22, thinking she might have assumed that I had walked ahead. But, in spite of a frantic search, I saw no one who even looked like her. As the queue of people boarding reduced, I thought to ask the attendant if my girlfriend had already boarded.

"Excuse me. Would you be able to tell me if a Sofia Sabina has already boarded?"

Looking down through her list, she said, "No, sorry – we are waiting for her and a Mr Christopher Dobson, though."

"Yes," I replied, "that's me."

"Well, sir, we are about to close this gate, so you must either board now or lose your flight, I'm afraid."

"Thank you," I said. "You carry on."

And the gate closed.

Walking slowly back to the main departure lounge, I was fraught with worry as to where on earth Sofia had gone. After all, it was pretty clear where we had been sitting. What should I do now? This was not an everyday occurrence surely. Stopping someone who looked half official, I enquired where the security office was. He gave me the directions, and off I went. What was I going to unravel?

"Come in," someone shouted as I knocked on the door. "How can we help?" said a kind-sounding lady.

I thought that I ought to take my time and explain everything slowly and clearly.

"Ah, you would be surprised how many of these incidents we get throughout the year," she said. "Some people just want to disappear," she added.

"Disappear? Why on earth would she want to disappear? We have a good fun life together, we love each other and . . ."

I couldn't make head nor tail of this.

"OK, let us take some details," she continued. "Where is your girlfriend from?" she asked.

"Colombia," I confirmed.

This did seem to stir some interest – why, I could not immediately think. A more senior-looking man came over to the desk.

"OK, Alice, I'll deal with the gentleman. Please follow me, sir," he said firmly.

Once again he asked me to go slowly through everything that had happened since arriving at the airport. Again I gave him the details, repeating what I had said in the other office. Then he asked me to follow him to a much bigger office, where there were banks of screens seemingly showing all public areas of the airport.

"You say your girlfriend has been studying here for the past three to four years?" he asked.

"Yes, that's right," I said.

"And she first came to the UK approximately five years ago?" he asked again.

"Yes, we met in Amsterdam on a city break. We travelled back to Birmingham together. She was on holiday, as I was, and we hit it off very well. To cut a long story short, we have been together ever since."

"OK, sir, please take a seat. This might take some time, but we have CCTV all around the airport, and people cannot just disappear," he confirmed.

This in itself was gratifying, but the situation was bloody worrying all the same.

The banks of screens were being watched by technicians. They covered every public part of the airport – boarding gates, lounge areas, passport control, security and even toilet areas (although only people going in and out).

"Now, this is where you say you were, waiting to see your boarding gate number come up," said a much younger man with 'Security Technician' on his badge.

"Correct," I enthused.

"Now, this is the timeline, you say, and we have cross-checked that against your flight departure time, etc."

"There! There!" I said, excitedly. "There is my Sofia, looking over at me before going to the toilet."

"Right," the voice said, "so let's see what happens now."

The frustrating thing was that Sofia could be seen making her way into the loo, clearly wearing her white blouse, red short skirt and high heels, but no one reappeared from the ladies with that description.

"What did she have in the bag, sir?" the man enquired.

"What? Oh, just normal hand-luggage stuff – a book or magazine to read on the plane, and her make-up bag, I think."

I could see that this saga was beginning to create a lot of interest, and another technician joined the merry band of people trying to locate Sofia.

Two and a half hours later, John Spicer, one of the technicians, beckoned me into another room, where they explained that they thought they had a lead on finding Sofia.

"How well do you know your girlfriend?" they asked.

"Why?" I replied.

"Please answer the question," they insisted.

"Well, all I really know is that Sofia comes from Bogotá. Colombia, she is twenty-five years old and has had a difficult life, losing her parents at an early age."

Once again I slipped into a trance, thinking I might have missed something.

Sofia lived in an area known a La Candeleria, approximately fifteen miles from El Dorada International Airport. I believe it to be a tough area. Having lost her parents, she had to find a job so she could feed and clothe her two brothers and sister. Work was at that time difficult to find, but she managed to get a bartender job in José's Bar in Chapinero. This enabled her to look after her family, save some money (which later was sufficient to apply to the university) and fly to England.

"Hello, Mr Dobson."

"Oh, sorry – I was trying to remember things so I could help give you better background information," I offered. "She brought up her brothers and sister and was trying to improve her life."

"OK, would it surprise you to know that Sofia Sabina is really

Sofia Fernandez, and that she flew out on a flight to Bogotá twenty minutes after the flight you were due on?" said Spicer.

"I'm sorry, but I do not understand," I said.

"No, it's not an easy one to understand, sir, but if you watch this clip of film you will see that Miss Sabina actually changed her clothes in the Ladies, put on a wig, changed her make-up and walked right in front of you, there." He pointed to the screen.

As I drove back home, I could not come to terms with the day's events. Skiathos seemed like a distant dream now. The security team said they would be back in touch with me as soon as they heard anything more.

This, I thought, would be in a day or so, but after two hours of being home there was a knock on the door.

"Mr Dobson, could we come in, please?"

"Who are you?" I asked.

"I am DC Mark Symons and this is DS Brian Lilly, airport police."

"You'd better come in," I said.

We walked into the lounge and sat down, and with bated breath I waited to hear the latest on the Sofia saga.

"Firstly, sir, thank you for all the information you gave us at the airport. You will be pleased to know that it all checks out. It has now been confirmed that Sofia Sabina – or Fernandez, to give her real name – is on the flight to Bogotá, which will land in the next thirty minutes or so. She will be watched by airport police when she arrives in Bogotá. Colombian Police suspect her of bringing drugs into Europe. Therefore when she lands nothing will happen to her, but she will be watched and her activities will be monitored," they explained. "When, or if, she decides to fly back to the UK is when the alarm bells will ring. She will then be challenged at the airport upon her arrival," DC Symons said.

DS Lilly then added, "Should she contact you, then we expect to be informed. Do you understand that?"

I meekly replied. "Yes."

As they left they chorused, "We'll be in touch."

When the policemen had been gone for a few hours, I decided to have an early night. So with Jameson in hand I slipped into bed and dropped off to sleep.

Suddenly the phone rang. What time was it? Bloody hell – 3 a.m. Who was calling at that ungodly hour?

"Hello."

"*Buenos dias*, Chris."

"Sofia, is that you?" I asked.

"*Si*, it is," she replied. "I can't talk for long, but I will send you an email and . . . I love you. *Ciao* for now."

'Oh, my God, at least she is safe, and . . .' I did not know what to think, so I made myself a coffee and poured another large glass of Jameson. Sleep was now impossible.

True to her word, thirty-six hours or so later Sofia sent a rather long email. She explained that, due to some debts one of her brothers had accrued, she had taken it upon herself to deal with the drug baron herself, agreeing to deliver certain packages to certain destinations to clear the debt. This was unusual as Diego Rodriguez was a ruthless operator. Once he had his claws into someone, that was it. However, she must have seen him on a good day. He had known her parents for years, so, as a favour to them, he did the deal with Sofia. One more delivery needed to be made and the debt would be clear. That was the agreement. This deal would be made soon, on a date which she would tell me about. She was aware that she was being watched, so she asked for help from me! What on earth could I do? The email ended with 'Be in touch.'

It was now seven thirty the following morning, and the phone rang again. I was beginning to feel a nervous wreck.

"Hello, Mr Dobson," said the voice.

"Yes?" I said.

"DC Symons. Have you heard anything yet?"

For whatever reason, I said, "No, not yet."

"OK, sir, we will be in touch again soon."

The call ended and I nervously went upstairs to shower and try to relax, but who could relax with all this going on? It was exhausting just to try and fathom out this wild story.

After four days I began to wonder about the events that had occurred, and I could have easily allowed myself to think it was all a dream. 'I should be lying on a lovely sandy beach in Skiathos,' I thought as my thoughts came back into focus. Then my mobile pinged and nervously I picked it up.

"Meet me at Schiphol Airport, Friday afternoon, landing at 4 p.m. from Panama. Note red hat and shoulder bag. Make sure you wear a disguise when we meet. Love you."

I was not sure I wanted to be part of all this. Was I going to end up just the fall guy? And this 'I love you' bit – I had actually been in love with Sofia for ages, but she had never expressed her love for me until now. Convenient or what? It all seemed like a very dangerous liaison.

It didn't take me long though to sort out my thoughts and my feelings for Sofia; so I began to look for flights to Amsterdam, and that was relatively easy: Friday morning, 10.35 a.m. with KLM. I'd be there by midday, so I'd have plenty of time to get to the terminal for the Panama flight due in at 4 p.m. But why Panama? After a moment or two I realised that because Sofia had to keep a very low profile, she had decided to fly back into Europe from a destination other than Colombia. Having booked and paid for my flight online, I suddenly thought about the disguise bit!

Our local charity shop was pretty upmarket, so I decided to try there first. I was quite lucky with the hat at £3.50, but as for the jacket and trousers – nothing. I moved on to a second-hand shop further into town, and found the ideal thing: an old tweed jacket with trousers, and my size too. Oh, and they had a walking stick.

Then there was the beard. A fancy-dress shop was only another half a mile up the road, so off I went, and acquired the necessary facial disguise. The flight into Schiphol took just over an hour, so I had time to familiarise myself with the layout of the airport before taking the next step. Nervously I made my way to the Gents and prepared myself. After ten minutes or so I looked in the mirror and was pleased with my handiwork. Off to Terminal Two I went, collecting a much needed drink and sandwich – oh, and a paper to complete my new image. By this time it was 3.35 p.m. I fidgeted a lot, pretending to read the paper I had bought, but I spent more time looking at the clock – 3.40, 3.43, 3.52 . . . could it be early? The arrivals board indicated it was on time.

It was 3.58 p.m. when I glanced above the paper at the runway and saw a Lufthansa 737 landing. My heart started to pound. Fifteen minutes or so later, passengers started to disembark, so I now kept a watchful eye on the trail of people coming off the plane. It seemed ages, but suddenly there she was – red hat and a shoulder bag – looking beautiful as always. I strolled towards her.

"Hi," she said.

"Lovely to see you," I added.

"Just stroll slowly towards the exit. Then we can talk," Sofia said.

First was passport control. I of course had to take off the beard to revert back to myself before this, but as it happened that was straightforward. Next was a taxi, and then we were off to a hotel and explanations.

We had a lovely room in the Marriot overlooking the city. We ordered a bottle of champagne and sat up in bed and started to talk. A lot of what Sofia told me I already knew, but I guess she wanted to tell the whole story so everything was out in the open.

Her mother and father had died in a car crash when she was very young, leaving the family short of money. In an attempt to help, one of her brothers was lured into delivering packages around the city. Of course the inevitable happened, and he got himself drawn into the network of drug running, etc. It didn't take long for him to owe a tidy sum of money, and the pressure grew on him to pay up. This is where Sofia became involved, because she wanted her family to have a free life, not pandering to the big and powerful. She managed to meet one of the leaders of this gang, a Diego Rodriguez – in fact he knew Sofia's parents – and she promised she would do what was necessary to pay off the debt as long as that was it. Rodriguez agreed out of respect for Sofia's parents.

"I have a package here in my case that I have to arrange collection or delivery of," Sofia told me. "Then I am done."

"What about us?" I thought to ask.

"Once we get back to the UK we can do whatever," she said.

"What would you like to do?" she asked.

"Well, firstly, how about Skiathos and those lovely warm seas and soft sand?"

"Good idea," she said.

Then I hesitated slightly. "Sofia, I have no ring to give you, but will you marry me? In other words, how would you like to get married there?"

"Do you mean that – really mean that?"

"Of course I do. I have loved you for quite a while."

Excitedly she said she would marry him, so some plans now had to be made.

"We have to get back home first, to make the arrangements, etc., but the UK authorities may be keeping an eye out for you, Miss Fernandez."

"Ah, you know my real name. I'm sorry about that. My passport says Sofia Sabina-Fernandez, so that will get me back, I guess," she explained. "Let's enjoy our evening, arrange for this collection, which I intend to leave at reception, and fly back."

Sofia felt great relief leaving the package at reception, and excitedly boarded the Flybe flight back to the UK, which was straightforward. We decided to keep away from the larger airports – hence our flight back was to Norwich.

As we landed my heart started to pound. However, we slipped through passport control and quickly hired a taxi to Nottingham.

A week went by, and the excitement rose as we printed our boarding passes and tickets for Skiathos take two. We couldn't wait for the following morning to come, but come around it did.

"Now, you are not going to disappear on me this time, are you?" I enquired.

"No way," she added.

As we prepared to board our flight to Skiathos, my thoughts went back to when we tried to do this the first time, especially when the doors of the plane closed and we knew we would soon be on our way. Relaxation! We needed that after the events we had been through. Then of course there would be the first steps into married life.

Skiathos was everything we wanted it to be. It was hot and the sea was lovely and warm. We managed to arrange, with help through the hotel, to have our wedding on the nearby beach. The hotel manager and a lovely lady called Ana who worked on reception agreed to be our witnesses. We treated them to a lazy lunch before we travelled back home.

Two weeks later we arrived back into Birmingham International Airport, relaxed, suntanned and happy. We hailed a cab to get back to the hotel, and within fifteen minutes or so we were loading the car for our journey back to the city – Nottingham. Wollaton is just off the A609, the main road into the city. Soon we could see the signs for 'Wollaton Hall, Gardens and Deer Park'. Nearly there! We could now see our house 100 yards ahead and started looking for a parking space. Our normal spot seemed to be taken by a strange-looking car with two men inside. As we approached the house, bags in tow, they got out and I suddenly had an awful feeling in my stomach that the events of the past weeks were going to continue to haunt us.

"Mr Dobson," said a voice.

"Yes, that's me," I answered.

"May we have a word, please?"

"Who are you?" I asked.

"Sorry to make this look official. I am Martin Lucas, Notts Constabulary, and it's about your mother, Mrs Violet Dobson."

"Oh, you'd better come in, then," I replied.

"I am sorry to be the bearer of bad tidings, sir, but your mother was involved in a car accident three nights ago. She drives an i20 Hyundai, I believe," he continued.

I just nodded.

"I am afraid she died from her injuries," he added.

"Oh, my God!" I exclaimed. "How did it happen?" I enquired.

"She was turning right off the A609 and a BMW hit her – side impact. An awful mess, and she died at the scene," he detailed. "This is not the news you want upon returning from holiday, sir," he said. Looking at Sofia, "Would you be Sofia Sabina?" he asked.

"I was. I am now Sofia Dobson," she replied.

"Ah, good job we caught you, then," he continued. "We have

been asked by the Dutch police to return this package to you. I think you know what is inside," he added. "It was left at the Marriot Hotel in Amsterdam," he explained.

"Do I?" Sofia said rather coolly. "Why don't we open it here and find out what is inside?" she confidently suggested.

With that, Lucas stood up. "OK, at this point I think we ought to take a trip down to the station."

Within a hour of arriving back from our holiday, we were on our way to the city police station.

'Great!' I thought.

Sofia glanced at me and whispered, "Don't worry – it is not what you think."

I was not sure what to add to that, but time would no doubt make things clear to me.

As soon as we arrived at the police station we were ushered into an interview room, where we were joined by a WPC and an Inspector Davis.

"So you wish this package to be opened," Davis said.

"Suits me," Sofia said, again very calmly.

Slowly and carefully the package was opened. I was expecting a powdery substance to flow on to the desk, and goodbye freedom! However, to everyone's surprise except Sofia's, six or seven gemstones fell out on to the desk.

"What is this?" Davis asked.

"Oh, these are emeralds from my home country of Colombia. We produce some of the best emeralds in the world. They are considered very valuable because of their deep-green colour. They come from the deepest part of the Andes," she explained.

Well, I was so proud and relieved at her response.

"What about Amsterdam?" Davis asked.

"I left them for a friend of my uncle to pick up," she said.

"Your uncle?" asked the Inspector, not knowing how to continue.

"Diego Rodriguez," Sofia boldly said.

You could have knocked me down with a feather.

"He is the drug lord, I believe," Davis countered.

"I have heard of him," said Sofia in reply, but my uncle is Miguel Diego Rodriguez – not the same person at all."

With that, the police left the room, only to return some ten minutes later looking very frustrated.

"You are both free to go, but we may need to question you again sometime in the future," said Davis.

Arriving home for the second time, I poured a couple of glasses of Shiraz, sat down opposite Sofia and frowned. She had a look of contentment on her face. In brief, she did have a package to deliver in Amsterdam, and that was left in the bathroom of our room to be collected. The other package was left at reception for her uncle's friend, which she would now have to return.

"So you totally confused them with two packages and two Diegos," I said.

"Yes," Sofia admitted, "and it seems to have worked. Do you think we could go and unpack now before we have something to eat?" she continued.

"How about we go over to Mr Man's for something to eat? After all, it is within walking distance, and we can relax over a few drinks," I suggested.

Sofia nodded. "I feel another holiday coming on," she said.

The following day we had to get a few things organised for my mother's funeral, which was likely to be in ten days' time. Visits to the church and various council offices seemed to take all day, and then there were a few calls Sofia had to make to finally get rid of the package. Most of this was accomplished in the day, and another glass of red was deemed necessary to draw a line under the whole saga.

The UK police never called again. They obviously heard nothing from the Colombian end; so the whole case must have been filed away, and Sofia Dobson was lost in the midst of a pile of paperwork. We were pleased also that none of this figured when Sofia went for an interview at Nottingham University, for a job she had applied for a month before. Ten days later she was offered the post of liaison officer, helping foreign students settle into the area.

Three Years Later

Government cuts were now beginning to take effect everywhere, and the education sector was no exception. Nottingham University had been constantly reviewing its budget for the year ahead, but still managed to retain all student services. However, this latest review with possible redundancies looked more serious.

"There is another meeting tomorrow," Sofia said, "all about the proposed cuts. I get the feeling something major is going to happen," she concluded.

"Well, you will be offered a financial settlement, I would think, and we can deal with it then," I suggested.

"Since receiving Uncle Diego's letter last week I have had a few ideas should the axe fall," Sofia confidently added. "But let us see what happens tomorrow."

I decided to come home early to hear what Sofia's outcome was likely to be. At four o'clock she came through the door and a smile came on her face when she saw me.

"How did it go?" I asked.

The smile quickly diminished and she proceeded to tell me that her department had another forty-eight hours to show savings and present them to the main board.

"This time next week I will know my fate," she said. "Anyway, I am not too worried as the latest email from Uncle Diego gives great hope for a new opportunity in the coffee business," she outlined.

"Wha-a-a-at? Coffee?" I enquired.

"Yes, coffee," Sofia said firmly. "There is a business at home in Colombia that wants to export coffee to the UK, and the Midlands is an ideal area in which to start," she explained. "Pour the tea and I will give you a fuller explanation," she added.

An hour later I was rather excited at the proposal that Sofia had outlined.

"So what is the name of this new company?" I boldly asked.

"Oh, Aroma Coffee," she proudly stated.

My next question was also confidently answered. "Where is this business likely to be based?" I asked.

"A lease is about to be signed for a unit at the newly constructed Nottingham 26 Business Park, on the way to Codnor," she explained.

Obviously a lot of planning had already taken place on this project.

Once again I ventured to come home ahead of Sofia to hear news from the university, and the result of the spending review. As I walked into the lounge I could see the floor was covered in paperwork – diagrams and floor plans.

"Oh, sorry – I did not hear you come in. Are you OK?" she asked.

"Yes, fine, thank you. But more to the point, are you?" I enquired. "What is the news from the review?" I questioned.

"Well, they have decided to merge our little department with another and Foreign Student Services will cease from the end of term," she explained. "The coffee business will be up and running by then," she confidently stated.

Four Weeks Later

After all the sad farewells everyone went their own way. Shortly after that Unit A at Nottingham 26 was being fitted out in preparation for the first shipment of coffee. Inside three days the shelves were filling with an array of coffee blends, soon to be delivered to bars, restaurants and supermarkets. Aroma Coffee had landed and was about to make a name for itself, and prove a worthwhile venture.

Aroma Coffee, thanks to Sofia's hard work, enabled us to sell our house in Woolaton Park and relocate to a property near Nottingham 26 on the Notts/Derbyshire border. It was a rural setting and an ideal location to bring up a baby, which was due in four months. By this time I was getting restless with my job at the planning department and decided to join Aroma – an experience I shall never forget.

THE ART OF DISGUISE AND DECEPTION 2

Aroma Coffee was now five years old and doing very well, and, as if to celebrate the event Sofia announced she was pregnant with our second child. Christina was four and growing up very quickly. She was enjoying her new friends at her playgroup and looking forward to starting school in Ripley, five miles away, very soon.

It was quite late when I arrived home, and I explained how the last shipment had been difficult to handle, due to poor packaging. So it was a case of all hands on deck and get it stacked away in time for the next delivery on Friday.

As tea was placed on the table I could tell there was something not quite right – something was on Sofia's mind.

"OK, what is it?" I asked.

"I do not know what you are talking about," she replied.

"You have something bothering you, I can tell. After all, I have lived with you a long time," I urged.

"OK, you win, but let us get Christina to bed and chat after."

"Fine by me," I added.

So we sat and enjoyed tea, just chatting about the day, but I was very curious as to what was to come.

Following a quick bedtime story, I dimmed the bedroom lights, kissed Christina on the forehead and tucked her in for hopefully a good night's sleep. As I came down the stairs I could not help wonder what was in store. I walked into the lounge, where two glasses of Shiraz were waiting on the coffee table. I collected one, eased myself into an armchair and waited for Sofia to join me. Picking up her wine glass, she lowered herself on to the settee and faced me. Then she proceeded to outline her thoughts all about the business.

"Chris, we have grown Aroma considerably over the past few years. However, now I am pregnant (which is wonderful) my contribution will naturally become less and less, and therefore we need additional help. So I have been thinking we need someone with knowledge of the coffee business – especially Colombian coffee and its origins – someone who speaks English and Spanish, is good with accounts and has a business brain."

"Hell's bells, that is some remit!" I said.

Sofia smiled.

"Sounds like you have someone in mind already?" I questioned.

"Yes, I have," she explained, "although she is not aware of it yet."

"What do you mean?" I asked with a frown.

"My cousin Isabella, who lives in Bogotá, has a degree in business admin and economics and has just finished her studies at the Isead Business School in the city. She also speaks English and Spanish, and therefore she fits the bill," she outlined.

"Well, you have done your research. How do you know she would be interested in coming here?" I enquired.

It appeared that Sofia and Isabella had been in touch regularly over the past months, and gradually the idea of this move came into Sofia's thoughts.

"This is a lot to take in, Sofia. Surely we could find someone in England, could we not?" I tendered.

"I am convinced", Sofia went on, "that Isabella would be a very good long-term investment for Aroma. I have been in touch with her recently via email, and I have given this whole thing a lot of thought. I wanted to run this past you, especially as we now have another child on the way. There is, though, one major problem," she stated.

"Oh?" I added with a grin on my face. Why did I think this was going to be simple?

"We need to go and find her, as it is nearly three weeks since we last emailed each other. She was moving to another part of the city and changing her email address. Then I discovered that she was caught up in a protest march which turned nasty – people simply complaining about high inflation, higher prices of everyday things, especially food, which is making it increasingly difficult to afford rents. Prices are going up and up and up," she explained. "Her last email made it clear that she wanted out and a fresh start somewhere with a stable job. She is longing to get away from the growing troubles around her."

"I suppose the next step is obvious," I said.

"Well, are you up for this, Chris?" she queried.

"Mrs Dobson, you are a very determined lady with a huge fighting spirit. How could I ever say no?" I confessed. "In the morning we will make the arrangements, but now let's enjoy our glass of Shiraz and have an early night," I suggested.

With my flight booked I ran through a few things with Sofia –incoming stock, sales figures and accounts to chase. Having packed my bag, and having final hugs with Christina, I hugged my Sofia, hoping that I would return with a new member of staff in a few days. It was a daunting trip, but one tinged with excitement too. I was about to leave the house when Sofia gave me her passport and a photo of Isabella.

Glancing at the photo, I said, "You two could pass for each other. You look like sisters."

Sofia smiled. "Many times in the past we have been mistaken for each other" was all she said.

I frowned and placed the photo and passport in my pocket. It was time to go – Gatwick next stop.

My drive to Gatwick was, as expected, busy.

'Where has all this traffic come from?' I asked myself.

I allowed plenty of time for my trip down south, as we say. Sometimes parking too can be a nightmare, but I was lucky and found the compound easily. I strolled into the main terminal building and found the BA desk to check in – Colombia, here we come! It was only four degrees in Gatwick, but the temperature would be an oppressive twenty-eight degrees in Bogotá.

'What a contrast!' I thought.

Fourteen hours or so later, I had arrived. I took a taxi into the city to the area known as Santa Ines, which was Isabella's last known address. There I hoped someone might nudge me in the right direction. After thirty minutes or so I found Isabella's address – a four-storey block of flats with six flats on each floor. I knew that Isabella's flat was number 7, and there I knocked and waited. After a few seconds I knocked again and this brought a response from a man in the next-door flat. In broken English he told me that Isabella had moved two weeks earlier.

"Do you know where she has moved to?" I asked.

"No" was his reply, but he pointed downstairs and said, "Flat 2 lady."

I thanked him and walked down to number 2. After two knocks a lady appeared, but her English was only as good as my Spanish. Her eyes brightened when I mentioned Isabella's name, but all she could do was point and say, "University."

Having studied a map of the city before flying, I had an idea of the location of this place of learning. I strolled through the streets, realising that I needed some refreshments or I would become dehydrated. I found a small back room of a place, where I could buy the necessary to sustain me in my quest to find the university. Twenty minutes or so later signs indicated that I was on the right track, but what on earth should I say when I got there? Time was also becoming a factor, and I needed to find a bed for the night. At the next junction there was a reasonable-looking hotel – pension-type – where I grabbed what they said was their last room. I bet they say that to everyone who calls in!

The university was another three blocks away. I decided to go to reception, where they might give me a clue where to find Isabella. I approached a middle-aged woman who was quite severe-looking. Trying to get even half a smile was difficult. Clearly she was wondering why I wanted this information, so I obliged with a story of a family bereavement. That changed everything. Her mood became sympathetic, and with a smile she suggested I sit and wait whilst she looked into the matter of Isabella Sanchez.

Half an hour or so later she was back at her desk. She beckoned me over and gave me a sheet of notepaper on which was written an address. I smiled, thanked her and went on my way feeling that I was making progress. However, I would have to wait till morning to continue my search as I was extremely tired. I was feeling exhausted after a very long day. First, though, I needed to call Sofia to update her on my findings.

Early morning sunshine greeted me as I pulled back the curtains of my room. I had slept surprisingly well, and I prepared myself for another day of searching for what would possibly be our next employee. A quick coffee and a croissant at a local bar set me up for the next few hours. Then I walked in the general direction of the address noted on the piece of paper handed to me by the lady in the reception of the university.

Santa Fé was a few miles across the city, but after thirty minutes or so I found Calle 27 – no street names here, just numbers. Once again it looked like an apartment building.

I approached the first person I came across and asked about Isabella, but the reply came back at me *"Lo siento, pero no entiendo."*

I later discovered that that meant they did not understand my question. Spanish I found was a very quickly spoken language, so I cringed when I could not engage in a meaningful conversation. I entered the building and found an office, where I enquired about Isabella and her whereabouts. Following a chat with someone who could understand and speak some English, I was told that she did live there, at flat number 10 as a matter of fact, but she was in police custody on a charge of unlawful protest and criminal damage. Oh, my God! What should I do now?

I managed to find out where the police station was. That obviously had to be my next port of call. I had about five minutes to think about what I was going to do next. Walking clears the mind, I am told. I needed to see Isabella to establish what had actually happened. I mean, were we about to employ a person with a criminal record? That, though, was the least of my thoughts as I walked up the police-station steps.

The police station was a large building, and I approached it nervously. As I walked to the main desk my eyes were met by an older man with a name tag – Detective Manuel Cortez. I was relieved that his English was quite good, and within a few minutes he had given me some information about Isabella. She was among about fifty people who had been taken into custody, and they were likely to be charged with a variety of offences, including violent conduct, threatening behaviour and disturbing the peace.

Cortez then admitted that Isabella had been charged only with disturbing the peace, and I sighed with relief.

"Would it be possible to see her?" I asked.

"Wait a moment, please, and I will arrange it," he said.

Twenty minutes later I was being escorted to a visitors' room, where I waited for Isabella to appear. Ten minutes later a door suddenly opened and in walked Isabella – a lovely-looking lady. And yes, she did look like Sofia.

"Isabella?" I asked.

"Yes, who are you?" she questioned.

The officer at the door kept a watchful eye on us as we settled at a table.

I kept my voice down: "I am Chris, Sofia's husband, from England," I explained.

A smile crept over her face.

"Why are you here?" she asked.

"Well, hopefully to take you back home with me and offer you a job, in brief," I offered.

The smile increased.

"I was not directly involved in this protest. I was just dragged along with it, ending up in here. I go before a judge next week," she told me.

My mind was working overtime, and without reason I suddenly came up with a plan which might help us all.

"OK, please just listen to me," I pleaded. "Sofia told me that you look very much alike, and now I have seen you I wholeheartedly agree. Where is your passport?" I asked.

"It is taped in an envelope under the only coffee table in my flat," she stated. "Why?" she added.

"I will try to retrieve it for you. Is there anything else that you specifically want or need from your flat to take with you to England?"

She gave me a list of things and I said goodbye. I also told her to start remembering Sofia's date of birth and full name, and that we had a family bereavement, and that she was very upset about it.

"Just create your own version of it all, and leave the rest to me," I said.

I was escorted back to the main reception area, where I found Cortez.

"Could I have a quiet word?" I asked.

"Of course. How can I help?" I told him of our family bereavement and that Isabella was very upset about it all, and I said that she really was only on the edge of this protest. The big question I asked was "What would it take to get her out of here?"

Cortez scoffed a little at the suggestion, but did not rule it out.

"I suggest you come and see me in the morning about midday and I will see what we can do," he told me.

I felt quite positive as I walked away from the police station, but now I had to go back to Isabella's flat and retrieve the things she wanted, including her all-important passport.

Arriving back at Isabella's apartment block I approached the lady at the front desk and asked her if I could borrow a key to get into her flat as Isabella needed some personal things whilst being detained. The lady kindly obliged. Up to her flat I went, wondering what I would find. After a few minutes I had found most of the things on my list. However, the underside of the coffee table did not reveal a passport. Now it looked as if plan B would have to be our way out of Colombia. After handing the key back to the lady, I made my way back to my hotel to put the remainder of my plan together.

Once I was back at the hotel, I called Sofia to update her on my progress. After three rings a little voice answered the phone: "Hello, Daddy," said Christina.

"Hello, Daddy's little girl. How are you?"

"I am fine. Do you want Mummy?"

"I do, please. See you soon."

Hearing what I had done, Sofia expressed approval and was excited that her long-term hopes might soon come to fruition, and particularly that I might be bringing Isabella back home with me.

The following day, as suggested, I returned to the police station and met Cortez. We shook hands and found a quiet place to talk. Then with bated breath I waited to hear his news.

"You asked me what it would take to release Señorita Isabella. Well, I have spoken to the local prosecutor's office and they have set a fine of $10,000 US," he stated. "Once payment has been received, she is free to leave," he added.

"OK, but please could you tell me, has her apartment been checked to confirm who she is and to confirm she is not an activist?" I enquired.

He smiled, nodded and said, "I think that is the case. Why do you ask?"

"Oh, the lady in the office thought that, and I wondered if it were true. Where and when would you like the money paid?" I enquired.

With a smirk on his face he stated that the money should be paid to him, and that he would ensure that everything was handed in to the correct office.

This all sounded very suspicious, but predictable. I came to the conclusion that the police had Isabella's passport and that not all the money would find its way to the correct office.

"Thank you, Señor. I will bring the money tomorrow about midday," I promised.

Cortez smiled and nodded and I believe he was thinking he would be a little richer tomorrow.

"Just one more thing," I said: "could I see Isabella once

more so I can tell her of our agreement and the family funeral arrangements? She was very close to her aunt," I pleaded.

"Of course," he said, and he called someone to arrange it.

Having advised Isabella of what was happening, I walked away from the police station towards my hotel. Passing a children's playground on the way, I stopped for a few minutes and imagined being home and cuddling my own little girl. 'Tomorrow, hopefully!' I thought.

I informed Sofia of the amount needed to be transferred. She would arrange for funds to be transferred into Citibank, which had a branch along the main street from where I was staying. My next job was to book two plane tickets to Gatwick. The airline turned out to be KLM for the earliest flight tomorrow, which was at 3 p.m. I hoped everything would flow to meet that time. Ah well, fingers crossed! I then packed my bag and paid my hotel bill, allowing of course for my stay that night. I thought that the easy bit was now done!

After a breakfast which I did not really feel like having, I thanked the receptionist and strolled to Citibank, a few streets away. It opened at 10 a.m. I was a little early, so impatiently I waited. Nervously I walked into the bank as the clock said 10 a.m. Upon discussion with a man at the desk, it took some time to ensure that the funds were in place.

"Did you want to open an account, sir? What about a high-interest account?"

"No, thank you, to both questions."

Inside I was screaming, 'Just hand over the bloody money. I want to go home.'

The cash was then placed into an envelope and off I marched to the police station. As I walked I went through a mental check of everything – cash, plane tickets, passports and Isabella's things, which were crammed into my case.

As I expected, a beaming Cortez was at the front desk waiting for me. He must have thought that Christmas had come early. We shook hands and I showed him the envelope, which he was keen to take from me.

But I held on to it, smiled and said, "Isabella."

Cortez returned my smile and, as if by magic, Isabella appeared. We gave each other a hug. I gave the envelope to Cortez, who was still smiling, and Isabella and I left the den of thieves, hailing a taxi as soon as we hit the street.

"Thank you, thank you" was all she could say.

'Well, we are not out of the woods yet,' I thought. 'We still have to get past security at the airport.'

"Have you remembered who you are?" I quizzed her, handing her Sofia's passport.

She frowned, took it and realised that hers was not to be found in her flat in Calle 27.

Approaching the airport, I turned to Isabella and said, "OK, this is the big test." I had a little smile on my face as I believed that Cortez was holding Isabella's passport and he obviously thought he would be richer and he would keep her in Bogotá for future reference.

Little did he know.

Inside the terminal building we found security and passport control.

"Boarding passes, please," a voice yelled.

'Oh, Lord, here we go!' I thought.

As we waited I was nervous as hell, but Sofia's stand-in sailed through with no questions asked. UK here we come!

Our flight back to Gatwick was on time, and we both managed to have a good sleep so when we arrived we were ready for the drive back up the M1 to home. It was very cold compared to sunny Bogotá, but it was dry, making driving conditions ideal for the journey home. If all went well we would be home in two or three hours. Isabella dozed off once or twice as we drove home, but awoke as we were about to turn off the M1 at junction 26. I now was getting very exciting at the thought of seeing my wife and daughter, and only a few minutes later we were turning into our road and slipping into our drive. Sofia ran out to meet us. There were lots of hugs and kisses and a few tears of joy too. Then there was a very excited little girl to deal with, who was not only pleased to see her daddy but delighted to meet her auntie for the first time.

I slumped into my favourite chair and all too quickly fell off to sleep. Sofia and Isabella chatted and chatted and chatted. Eventually Aroma Coffee came into the conversation, but it was all too much to take in. Isabella was clearly overcome by what had happened over the past few days. She had been rescued, and now there was a chance of starting a new life here with us. The day flew by and an early evening meal was arranged so we could have an early night – well, it was an early night for me at least. As for the girls, it was more chatting, which probably went on for several hours.

Some months later Isabella with a new passport and a work permit in hand, started working for Aroma Coffee, and what a difference she made! She settled into her new way of life very well, and now we were able to look at the next phase of Aroma Coffee. Exciting times for all.

THE ART OF DISGUISE AND DECEPTION 3

"Christina, Gabby, over here!" shouted Isabella as she picked up the two girls from school.

As they ran towards their auntie, their smiles grew wider.

"We didn't know you were collecting us today," yelled Christina excitedly.

"Ah well, that was a nice surprise, then," Isabella said, tucking them into their car seats.

As they pulled out into the traffic, Isabella explained that their mummy and daddy wanted her to pick them up as they would be back from work later than normal. "So what would you like for tea?" she asked.

"Can we have boiled eggs and soldiers?" they chorused.

"OK – no problem."

As they neared home, "Where have you been today?" asked Christina.

"I have been to Chatsworth House," explained Isabella. "Have you two been?"

"Mummy and Daddy have taken us a couple of times, I think," explained Gabriela.

With boiled eggs and the soldiers finished, the girls climbed the stairs to play before bath time and a bedtime story. Ten minutes later the front door opened and in walked Sofia and Chris.

"Hi," Sofia shouted. "Everything OK?" she continued.

Isabella came to meet them, and a hug and a kiss later they moved into the kitchen. Suddenly there was a thunder of steps on the stairs, and two young children came rushing towards their mum and dad for hugs.

"Have you had a good day?" they asked.

"Yes, we have, and Auntie Izzie collected us from school," they shouted excitedly.

Smiling, Sofia and Chris just nodded and said, "We know."

The clock eased past 6 p.m. and Chris asked as it was TGIF – Thank God It's Friday – would they like a drink?

Nodding with enthusiasm, Sofia and Isabella suggested G & T's would be good.

"So where have you ventured today, Izzie?" questioned Chris.

"I have been to Chatsworth House and I have joined the National Trust."

"Oh, well done you! So you think you will stay around for a while, then?" teased Chris.

I love it here," Isabella said. "How is the work at the warehouse progressing?" she asked.

"Well, it should all be complete by this time next week," Chris suggested, pouring the tonic on to the gin.

"That should make a real difference," Sofia said.

"Sure will," added Chris, bringing in the two drinks.

As they moved into the lounge to enjoy their drinks, Isabella picked up some post and gave it to Sofia, noting at the same time that there was a letter there from Colombia.

"I wonder who this is from?" questioned Sofia, slicing open the long-distance letter.

A few sips later, with Sofia still engrossed in the letter, Chris and Isabella looked at her and Chris said, "Care to share?"

"Oh, sorry," she offered, "Uncle Diego has written, and . . . well, you can read the details," she suggested.

Sitting together, Chris and Isabella read the letter. Once finished, the letter was placed on the table and frowns emerged on their faces.

"Why?" Sofia asked.

"Pretty obvious, I think," offered Chris. "Aroma Coffee is nearing its tenth year, and he has not seen the girls, so maybe a little celebration is due!"

"You could be right," suggested Sofia. "But . . . I am not totally convinced," she said, shaking her head. "He also says he will only be staying a few days before flying on to Amsterdam to see his long time-friend, Martyn van Bastin. But why is he going to see him?" Sofia enquired.

Whilst Sofia pondered over Uncle Diego's visit Isabella gave the two girls a quick bath and prepared them for bed before reading them a short story. Chris and Sofia then tucked the girls in, and within a few minutes all was quiet.

"Now for some tea," Chris whispered. "So Diego's itinerary, to be confirmed, is arriving here next Friday, spending the weekend with us and flying to Amsterdam on the Tuesday from Birmingham," outlined Chris. "Perhaps we could book a table at The Dog for, say, Saturday evening, and have a little celebration there?" he continued.

"Sounds fine," Sofia said. "I will leave that with you, then," she confirmed. "Will you arrange babysitters? I assume Mary across the road would step in. I'll check."

The Following Friday

The KLM flight was on time, which Chris was very pleased about. Many people were at the arrival gate greeting friends and family. Eagerly looking towards the automatic door, Chris soon picked out Uncle Diego. They greeted each other with a hug and a few words,

"Good to see you, Christopher. How are you?"

"I am fine, Diego. Now let us pick up your bags and make our way home."

Gatwick was busy most of the time, but seemed extremely busy now. Bags in hand, they found the car, loaded up and called Sofia to say all was well – Diego had arrived and they were about to leave Gatwick.

Chris realised that Diego must be tired after his long flight, so did not engage in too much conversation. However, Diego seemed quite alert and asked about Aroma and how things were going.

After explaining the progress that was being made and the plans which they had, Chris just asked, "How are you, Diego? Are you keeping well?"

"Why do you ask, Christopher?" he enquired.

"Well, I must be honest: Sofia and I are a little concerned about you, coming over and then flying off to Amsterdam. We wonder if all is OK?"

"Ah, I had a feeling Sofia might think there must be a good reason for my visit. She has an enquiring mind. I have several things to talk to you about – Isabella, too – some good, some not so good. Christopher, I am seventy-two years old and I have smoked all my life – well, up until I was told by my doctor and consultant to stop in the university hospital at Santa Fé, in Bogotá. I have had a hard, but good, life and all I want to do now is to ensure that I help Aroma, Sofia and Isabella as best I can. I don't think, Christopher, that I will be able to make this journey again, if you understand me," Diego explained.

"Oh, Sofia thought there was some underlying reason for you coming over," Chris outlined.

"What gave me away?" Diego asked.

"Well, I think it was your onward flight to Amsterdam which raised the question why?"

"Ah," Diego acknowledged, nodding.

"Is there nothing that can be done?" asked Chris.

There was no answer, and when Chris glanced across at Diego he saw he had dropped off to sleep.

'A quiet drive ahead!' he thought to himself.

The miles passed by and soon Chris picked up the sign for junction 26 and home. The change of speed disturbed Diego's sleep, and a quick rub of his face freshened him up for the greeting he would inevitably receive. One more turn and number 17 was in sight. As the car came to a stop Sofia and Isabella ran out to welcome them. There were a few tears of joy and excitement as they all went inside for a welcome cuppa.

As expected, there were more questions than answers regarding Diego's visit. However, Chris found himself concentrating on what Sofia might be keen to ask as he wanted to prevent certain things being discussed tonight. Thankfully she must have read his concerned look, so no delicate questions were forthcoming this side of bedtime.

With the lights switched off, Sofia and Chris climbed the stairs to bed, but as soon as the door closed Sofia seized upon the opportunity to interrogate Chris with a barrage of questions. He quietly told her about Diego's condition and the reason for his visit at this time. She was naturally upset at hearing this news, but would have to wait until the morning to discuss things further.

As Chris stirred from a good night's sleep all he could hear was giggling, and not from where he would have expected it to come. Dressing gown on, he slipped into the hall and found two excited little girls sat on Diego's bed telling stories about their school and their friends.

"What are you two doing?" he asked, peering around the door.

They were surprised to hear his voice, and turned around quickly to give good reasons why they were chatting away to Diego.

"It has been fun, Christopher, to listen to their stories," admitted Diego.

"Did you sleep well?" Chris asked.

"I did" was all he could manage as his attention was taken once again by the two delightful girls.

A visit to Nottingham 26, Aroma's office, was the first thing after breakfast – a visit which Sofia and Isabella were more than pleased to undertake. After all it was his brainchild. After the guided tour, which certainly impressed Diego, he wanted to see the offices – not to see the set-up, but to have the chance to talk to Sofia and Isabella about a few things.

"I need to explain a few things to you both here in the quiet. I appreciate that you are wondering about my visit, and why I am going to fly on to Amsterdam on Tuesday. So let me explain. I have several times over the past few months been to the university hospital in Santa Fé for tests, and I have been told that I have a tumour on my lung, probably brought about by smoking all my life. The prognosis is not good, and I can tell you now that I do not think I will be able to make this trip again," Diego outlined.

"Wha-a-at? You mean . . ." said Sofia.

Diego nodded. "I am afraid so, but honestly I have had a good life, Sofia, and all this gives me so much pleasure. And of course you can now see why I want to go to see my lifetime friend Martyn in Amsterdam, to tell him the news too," explained Diego.

Some hugs and tears followed. All this was a lot to take in, but take it in they did." Martyn and I first met in New York nearly thirty years ago, and we have remained friends ever since. He is into rare stones, including diamonds, and he has always had an eye for Colombian emeralds. He is a lovely man," he added.

"But is there nothing – no treatment – that they can offer?" pleaded Sofia.

"I am having a course of chemotherapy when I go back. That may help, but I am not too optimistic," Diego confirmed.

They drove the few miles back home in a somewhat sombre mood.

Returning from the visit, it was time for some lunch. Chris had booked a table at The Dog pub and restaurant for 7 p.m. and requested a quiet table, if possible, so they could talk. A drive around the Derbyshire countryside filled the afternoon, and it would soon be time to get ready for their evening out.

"Who is babysitting, Mummy?" asked Christina.

"Mary from down the road," explained Sofia.

"Oh, yippee! She's fun," she said with a broad smile on her face.

"You be good" was their mother's warning.

"We will" was the reply.

The short car ride to The Dog only took twenty minutes, with the car park on arrival looking quiet, as was the pub inside. Diego made it clear that this was his treat. No one argued. Menus in hand, everyone studied the delights being offered, and, after what seemed like ages decided to order. As the waitress walked away Diego raised a glass and wanted now to explain something else to them – something they might like to hear, or not.

"You may remember Alberto Llano and his tea plantation. He died many years ago, but his son Manuel continues running the business. He has two sons, and he thought that one might be interested in carrying on after him, but sadly one moved to Brazil to work as an accountant and the other moved to Argentina to manage a shipping line. This has left him with nobody to run the export part of his business. He is not ready to retire yet, but he wants some of the weight taken off his shoulders. He wishes to strike an exclusive deal with a company in the UK, and he needs someone who knows the country, etc.," he explained.

He could see that Sofia wanted to ask a question, but he held up his hand before she could speak, and added, "And that, if you want, could be you."

With that, the starters arrived, so quiet returned to the table, but momentarily. Sofia was anxious to ask many questions, the main one being if they wanted to go ahead what would they have to do?

"Ah," Diego said, "what is it you say? There is no gain without pain," he added.

This time it was Isabella who asked, "Pain? What pain?"

"Someone will have to go to Bogotá to finalise the agreement. Manuel wants to shake hands with someone and trust that person. He is from the old school. He depends on people, not emails. Yes, emails will be needed once things are up and running, but first he needs to meet you in person," Diego informed them.

There was silence as now the main course was being served.

Having said very little up until now, Chris said, "The problem, Diego, is we are all – or I think we are all – marked men in Bogotá. I did a deal with the devil to get Isabella out of Colombia, and she used Sofia's passport. They may still be keeping an eye out for Sofia for the drug problem all those years ago, so this will take some thinking about."

"It will be fine," enthused Sofia. "We have done it once; we can do it again," she continued.

Frowning, Chris looked at his wife and said, "We have two young children to consider, Sofia, before we go charging off to South America."

"I realise that," she admitted.

The main course was then enjoyed with little else being said.

With their heads full of ideas, an early night was called for. However, Chris and Sofia poured a Jameson and sat in the kitchen throwing around a few thoughts and ideas.

"OK, who is going to go? Where are we going to store this tea, and who is going to sell it?" Chris asked impatiently.

"All these things we can get over, Chris. It is a case of do we want it? The business bit fits – coffee and tea, and not any old tea. This is specialist loose-leaf tea. So I think marketing or delivering it would not be a problem. Exports of tea from Colombia are not huge – I think only about four and a half per cent of the total per year, and the Llanos Company is a small part of that, so we need to put this into perspective," she concluded.

"The last time we had this sort of discussion, Sofia, you had someone up your sleeve – namely, Isabella – but we do not have that now, do we?" Chris questioned.

"No" was all Sofia could muster, her mind working overtime in an effort to solve this problem.

The lovely evening meal at The Dog and a couple of glasses of wine were the recipe for a good night's sleep. After a few pages of his book, Chris slipped off to sleep quite easily. However, he suddenly was being shaken to wake up. Bleary-eyed he realised it was not a dream, but Sofia.

"What on earth is wrong?" he muttered. "Is everything OK?" he further asked.

"Yes, fine" was Sofia's reply.

"Then what the hell are you waking me for?" he questioned.

"Listen – I have an idea about going back to Colombia."

"Couldn't it wait until morning?" Chris asked.

Cringing, Sofia said, "Sorry about the time, but . . ."

"OK, let's hear it – then perhaps I can go back to sleep," Chris conceded.

Thirty minutes later he was wide awake and buzzing with what Sofia had told him. Once she had stopped, he took a deep breath and went and made some tea – English tea. Coming back into bed, he asked Sofia to run her idea past him again, but slowly. It seemed to make more sense the second time around.

"OK, can we go through this again in the morning? Then we can start putting the plan together with the iPads on hand to check details."

Sofia agreed, and they cuddled in to hopefully catch a couple more hours of sleep.

After breakfast the girls took Diego for a walk, which gave Sofia, Chris and Isabella a chance to chat things through and examine the plan they had hatched in the early hours. We considered that leaving the country on a false passport is the least of our worries, a small matter as offences go; so, Isabella, would you remain in the UK to look after Aroma and look after the girls?"

This she was pleased to do.

"So what are you two going to do?" she enquired.

"Well, I need your passport – as insurance, of course," said Sofia, looking at her cousin. "If – and it is a big *if* – we are likely to be monitored on arrival, then perhaps we should fly individually, Chris into Bogotá and I will go into Medellín, which is a smaller airport where they may be less attentive as to who is arriving. If we could meet Manuel on the outskirts of Bogotá I think that would be very helpful. Perhaps we should ask Diego to arrange that. Then", she continued, "we could both fly back from Medellín or switch airports if necessary."

"Sounds easy, but . . . are you sure?" Isabella asked.

"Well, let us see what Diego thinks when he comes back. If he thinks it could work, we can arrange details when we look more closely at flights and hotel, etc."

Returning from his walk with the girls, Diego sat and listened to their proposal. Nodding in the process, he said he would speak to Manuel and see what he could arrange.

After a couple of hours looking at flights and hotels they felt more at ease with the prospect of going back to South America, and getting out again, without any trouble.

The following morning Diego appeared in the kitchen with a smile on his face.

"I have spoken to Manuel and he is happy to meet you. He suggests the Europa Hotel in Medellín. He has a favourite restaurant close by called Torres, where he would like to take you by ways of celebration, if all goes well. All you have to do is email him when your flights have been confirmed."

Ten days had passed since Diego had left them for Amsterdam, and in the meantime he had flown back to Colombia. They would not see him again on this trip, but email or phone they certainly would. Christina and Gabriella were not too bothered about their mum and dad flying off somewhere, as long as their Auntie Isabella was there for them. Sofia and Chris said their goodbyes and drove down to Gatwick for their flights to Medellín and Bogotá. Sofia was the more nervous, but Chris kept having thoughts of bumping into Detective Cortez.

After a simple taxi to the end of the runway, a sudden thrust and acceleration saw them speed down the said runway and lift into the sky. Chris was going to arrive in Bogotá and get a connecting flight to Medellín. He should then meet up with Sofia hours later.

Sofia sat wondering about this trip as the same sudden burst of acceleration lifted her into the London skies. She had both passports, so if things did get a little sticky she could when needed become Isabella. In a few hours' time she might be tested, but for now sleep would be a good idea.

Chris arrived in Bogotá on time and nervously approached the information desk to find out the gate number for the flight to Medellín. He was directed to gate 17 and off he went, arriving in plenty of time. His documents were checked and so was his passport. Neither caused a stir. His flight would take approximately two and a half hours, so he prepared for the next stage of this trip. Would there ever be a time when he and Sofia would come to Colombia without all this cloak-and-dagger stuff?

Sofia arrived in Medellín thirty minutes late, and she too nervously approached the passport control desk. Seconds later she was collecting her baggage and hailing a taxi to the Alexis Park Hotel.

The city was indeed busy, and any thought of a quick thirty-minute ride vanished when the traffic came to a stop due to an accident. Chris now realised that his flight was making its approach into the airport. He would be very relieved to catch up with Sofia. Now he wondered what might be in store for him.

A smiling officer greeted him at passport control, asking, "What is the purpose of your visit, sir?"

"I have a business meeting to attend tomorrow, after which hopefully I will be returning to England," Chris replied.

Then the man received an internal call, which caused a little panic.

Still smiling, the man at the desk asked Chris if he would step into a side room.

"Why?" asked Chris.

"This will not take a minute or so," the man insisted.

Now deeply concerned, Chris wondered what was coming next. Escorted to the side room, Chris took a breath as the first person he set eyes on was none other than Detective Cortez.

"Mr Dobson, how are you today?" the Detective said, leaning forward to shake hands.

"I am well, thank you," Chris replied. "But why are you here?" he enquired.

"I was transferred here two years ago. I usually study the passenger manifest of incoming flights, and – surprise, surprise! – Mr Dobson is here again. So I just wanted to say hello," he explained.

Chris sighed a huge sigh of relief.

"How is Miss Sanchez?" Cortez then asked with a big smile on his face.

Chris, not sure how to respond, decided to offer a small smile of his own, and he said, "She is safe and well, thank you."

"Good," said Cortez. Then he added, "Please don't try to fool us like that again, Señor Dobson. You were aiding a person to travel with a false passport, which is an offence in every country – not just Colombia."

Chris nodded and waited.

"Have a pleasant trip," Cortez then added.

With that the door opened and Chris left, breathing heavily.

Outside now, and with his heart pounding, Chris hailed a taxi and thankfully soon found himself on the way to the Alexis Park Hotel. Chris suspected he was being followed, but thankfully, as the taxi pulled into the hotel driveway, the following unmarked car passed by. Sofia who was waiting in the hotel lobby was very relieved to see her husband.

"Where have you been?" she pleaded.

"Let us have a drink in the bar and I will tell you all," Chris said.

"Ah, so there was something!" she concluded.

Over a couple of beers Chris explained his brush with Cortez, and the conversation they had, and he told her he thought he had been followed.

"What sort of car was it?" Sofia asked.

"Well, it was unmarked, black, dark windows in the back, and two guys inside. That is as much as I can say!" exclaimed Chris.

"That would be Cortez's men, I guess," she said. Continuing, she questioned how many nights they had booked the room for.

Chris said that when they had booked it they had explained that they did not know how many nights they would want to stay for, and the hotel said they could have it on a night-by-night basis.

"Why do you ask?" he asked Sofia.

"I'll explain later. Just go to the desk and say you are paying for tonight only. Say we have had an urgent call changing our plans."

"Have we?" Chris asked.

"No, Chris. Just do it, and I will explain after," she said impatiently.

Whilst Chris was at the desk, Sofia was on her phone, and she was saying thank you when Chris came back to her.

"Was that OK?" she asked.

Chris nodded, then asked whom she was speaking to on the phone.

"I have booked us into the Park Hotel for tonight and tomorrow night, so let's get a taxi out of here – via the rear entrance if possible," she announced.

"Why?" Chris asked again.

"Because if you were followed, then, take it from me, they will follow us all the time. They may even call in and cause problems – papers here, passports there – so we need to move now," Sofia excitedly explained.

After hailing a cab at the rear of hotel, they were fifteen minutes later booking into the Park Hotel, and apparent safety. They threw their bags on to the bed and went off to find the hotel restaurant. Neither had much of an appetite, but enjoyed what they ate. After the meal an early night was called for, but not before a quick call to Isabella to say all was well, and to check that the girls were behaving.

After breakfast and a call to Manuel to confirm all was OK, they strolled through Amazon Park, which was looking beautiful in the morning sunshine. Coming out of the park, they came to a set of lights on a busy junction.

Whilst they were waiting, a voice shouted, "Sofia, is that you?"

Sofia did not immediately turn around, but slowly did so when the voice shouted again, sounding more friendly now.

'What is coming now?' Chris wondered.

The person who had shouted then ran towards Sofia, and screams of joy followed as the two women hugged each other for what seemed like ages.

As they broke away from each other, Sofia, smiling, turned to Chris and spluttered, "Chris, this is my sister Maria."

The fact that Maria was in a police uniform seemed to pass them by momentarily as they moved back inside the park and found a seat.

"What is all this?" Sofia asked, pointing to Maria's uniform.

Maria then explained that their brothers had moved to Mexico, and she needed to earn a living as José's Bar had closed. "The police force was advertising, so I applied, went to police college, passed all the necessary exams and the rest is history. I was posted to traffic here in Medellín some four years or so ago."

There were of course many questions, which quickly followed, but not all of them could be answered then. Realising the time, Chris nudged Sofia and pointed to his watch. After explaining to Maria that they had to go, they made arrangements to have dinner together that night at 7 p.m., when time would allow for explanations, etc.

The meeting with Manuel Llanos in the Hotel Europa went smoothly. Diego had obviously provided Manuel with most of the information, and it seemed all Chris and Sofia's concerns were diluted to nothing.

"You have a sound business, Sofia," Manuel stated.

"Well, it has taken some time and a lot of effort to get where we are," she confirmed.

"I wish my sons were able to carry on the export side of the family business, but grander things beckoned, I am afraid," he explained sadly.

After thirty minutes or so Manuel eased some documents from his briefcase and outlined the contents, which were brief and to the point.

"If you both are happy, perhaps we could all sign this," he said, pointing to the contract. "Then shall we go and have some lunch?" he asked with anticipation.

All three added their signatures, smiled, rose from the settees and shook hands. Aroma now was to become a huge business with coffee and loose-leaf tea sales throughout the UK.

"I think we should set up a trading name in the UK for this new venture," Chris chipped in.

"Good idea," said Manuel, nodding. "How does Te Negro sound?" he offered.

"Where did that come from?" asked Sofia, smiling.

"Not sure really. It just came to me."

"Te Negro sounds good to me," said Sofia, rising from her chair. "Our management structure will need looking at, but we can talk about that later."

A brief walk around the corner found them at Bar Torres, a quaint-looking restaurant. It was quite busy. However, as soon as they entered, Manuel was directed to a reserved table towards the back. Chris glanced around – why, he had no idea – and to his amazement he saw Cortez just leaving. Their eyes met and they both smiled briefly. Cortez left the building.

Chris sat down and shared a glass or two of bubbly before ordering food, and then they all enjoyed a very tasty lunch. Finishing their meal with a brandy, Manuel confirmed that he was delighted to have struck a deal with Aroma, and he said he looked forward to visiting Chris and Sofia sometime in the future.

As they made their way back through Amazon Park, Sofia stopped at a park bench and urged Chris to do likewise.

"What is it?" she asked.

"Cortez was in the restaurant. He was actually leaving as we sat down. He is watching me all the time, I feel," Chris slowing said.

"Ah, I thought something was wrong," she murmured.

As they got up to walk a little more, there he was again, walking towards them.

"We meet again, Mr Dobson – and Isabella Sanchez too. Good to see you are OK. I need to see your passport, please, Miss Sanchez," Cortez smugly asked.

"This is bordering on harassment," said Chris.

But, not for the first time, Sofia took over: "Well, Detective Cortez, you are welcome to look at my passport [passing it over to him confidently]. As you can see, I am Sofia Dobson, now a UK citizen," she added.

Cortez took a quick look at the document and handed it back to her, adding, "Thank you. Have a safe flight back to the UK."

Clearly smarting from this encounter, he quickly marched on, having been thwarted again because of the two passports.

At 6.45 p.m. Chris and Sofia made their way to reception and waited for Maria. On time, fifteen minutes later, Maria arrived glowing, with a broad smile.

"I cannot believe this is happening," Maria said. "Please tell me everything," she continued.

"Well, there is not enough time to go through everything, but here goes!" Sofia exclaimed.

Maria listened in amazement, smiling and at times gasping at the twists and turns that had occurred in Sofia's life over the past ten years or so.

"What about you?" Sofia asked. "When I came over last you were running José's Bar."

Again Maria took centre stage and explained how her life had changed after José's Bar closed. "I needed to do something, but what, I did not know. Then I found they wanted police officers in Medellín. Of course I had to go through the training programme, and then twelve months ago I became a *subteniente*. You were gone to Europe, somewhere, and the boys had moved away, so I thought, 'Why not?' So here I am," she proudly outlined.

In between all this news, a lovely meal was enjoyed. The two sisters had been reunited by pure luck.

At the end of the evening Maria shed some tears. "When will I see you again?" she choked.

"You could pay us a visit sometime," Sofia suggested.

Her mood brightened and Maria nodded, saying that she would make every effort to do that before too long.

"We fly back tomorrow," said Chris.

"Why don't you have breakfast with us before we go to the airport?"

"That would be wonderful. Actually I am on holiday for the next ten days off, so I could take you to the airport afterwards," Maria excitedly suggested.

"Tomorrow it is, then," Chris said.

It had been an eventful day in which another business opportunity had been successfully negotiated. Aroma was to have a sister company, Te Negro, to work alongside. But for now a nightcap was called for to celebrate, before their beds beckoned.

Breakfast the following morning was a simple affair. When it was time to go, Maria drove to the airport; and she plucked up courage at the last minute to ask if there was a seat on the plane could she come back with them now?

"Are you serious?" Sofia asked.

"Yes" was the simple reply.

"Well, over to you, then," her sister replied, jumping for joy.

At the KLM desk, Maria chatted to the assistant and requested a single ticket to the UK. Next Chris and Sofia could see Maria paying some money using her credit card.

"It looks as if our house is going to become very crowded," Chris observed.

The trip back into Gatwick was uneventful. Finding the car and the drive to the Midlands proved equally straightforward. Maria had spent some time asleep and woke to find Chris exiting the motorway, not far from home. Not for the first time there were joyous scenes in the Dobson household. Isabella, who had no idea Maria would be arriving back with Chris and Sofia, yelled with excitement. The next few hours developed into a mass catch-up of the past few years, at which point everyone was more than tired. Sleep was calling.

Sofia, though, did not drop off to sleep easily. She found herself planning and scheming. Could Maria deal with Te Negro? Would she want to leave the police force in Medellín? These questions and others would have to be aired, but it all added up to an exciting future.

THE ART OF DISGUISE AND DECEPTION 4

Farewell, Diego

It was a late start the following morning – well, apart from Isabella, who dealt with getting the girls ready and off to school. Chris rose first, followed by Sofia, and immediately he knew she had something on her mind.

But before he had a chance to ask, she came right out with what she was thinking: "If – and it is a big *if*, I admit – Maria was interested—"

Before she had a chance to complete her sentence, Chris had put his hand up to stop her.

"Totally agree," he said.

"With what?" she exclaimed. "You don't know what I was going to say," she added.

"I do. I have known you a very long time, and you were going to say about offering Maria a job, looking after Te Negro," Chris said proudly. "Oh, and good idea, by the way!" he continued.

Sofia was rather taken aback by the statement Chris had just made, and asked herself how he knew what she was going to say.

Having showered and dressed, Sofia then made her way downstairs to find Chris making coffee.

"So do you think it would be a good idea?" Sofia asked.

"What would be a good idea?" said a voice coming down the stairs.

"Good morning, Maria. Did you sleep well?" asked Chris.

"Very well, thank you," she replied as she embraced her sister. "So what would be a good idea?" Maria continued after her hug.

"Let's sit down and have some breakfast first," Sofia suggested, which they did.

Within a few minutes the back door opened and in walked Isabella from the school run.

"Everything OK at school?" enquired Sofia.

"Fine" was the reply.

Another cup was poured and the four settled down for a chat.

Chris, having moved all the breakfast things, was first to broach the subject of Te Negro. "Maria, are you happy with your job with the police force in Medellín?"

"Well, what a question to ask a girl at this time of the morning! Let's say there is little else on offer. And, most importantly, I get paid every week, so what is not to like about it? Why do you ask?" she enquired.

Sofia stepped in first this time with "Well, we need someone to run Te Negro, to liaise with Manuel Llanos and deal with this new business of ours."

"OK, not an easy question, then!" smiled Maria.

The next hour or so was filled with how, what, where and when. This was followed by Isabella suggesting that she and Maria have a 'girlie' rest of the day.

"I will think about what you have said," said Maria as she and Isabella left the house thirty minutes later.

Whilst enjoying their day out, Maria seized the opportunity to talk to Isabella about the offer mentioned over breakfast.

Isabella was firm with her thoughts: "After all, I have settled very well here in the UK and I don't envisage going back to Bogotá in the near future. But not everyone can settle that easily," she continued.

Pondering over Isabella's comments, Maria admitted that she did not think she was ready to leave her Colombia yet, but would give it more thought during the next twenty-four hours.

Arriving back at the house, and with Chris pouring an early evening drink, Maria and Isabella eased themselves on to the settee and sipped their glass of Pinot Grigio.

"Cheers!" they said.

With that, Sofia arrived back with the children, having collected them from some friends they had visited after school. Whilst the two girls took themselves upstairs for an early night, Sofia slipped into an armchair and poured a cold glass of vino too.

"Did you order the takeaway?" Chris asked Sofia.

"I most certainly did – about 6.30 p.m., I think."

"Great! I am feeling quite hungry," said Maria.

"Me too," added Isabella.

With that, the doorbell rang and the Chinese takeaway had arrived. Plates and serviettes were all ready as dishes were opened and food served.

Some forty-five minutes or so later, and with everyone having enjoyed the delights of the takeaway, the phone rang. Chris was the one who answered it, and he immediately realised it was an international call.

"Hello," he said.

"*Hola. Esta Sofia Dobson ahi, por favor?*"

Understanding some Spanish, Chris said, "Yes, she is here. One moment, please," and he motioned to Sofia that the call was for her.

"Hello. Sofia speaking."

"*Gracias. Soy la hermana Lucianna Martinez, Sante Fé Hospital, Bogotá.*"

Sofia continued to listen, asking a few questions as the conversation progressed. Minutes later, the phone was slowly replaced on the table, and she made her way back to the others in a rather sad mood.

The silence in the room was deafening. Who was going to ask first? Chris realised something was seriously wrong and rose to cuddle his wife, who now was in floods of tears.

"What is it, Sofia?" asked Maria.

Over the next thirty minutes or so the phone call was relayed to everyone: Uncle Diego had been taken into hospital; he was very poorly; the tumour had not responded to the chemotherapy he had been receiving, and the hospital thought they should know.

"Meaning?" asked Chris abruptly.

"I suppose if we wish to go and see him, with his time running out, now would be the time," Sofia outlined. "And Maria and I are his next of kin – there is no one else."

Isabella was the first to state what was obvious really: "Well, we can't all go, as much as we would want to."

Maria then added, "Well, I have at some stage got to go back. I can change my flight and go back with Sofia if that is OK?"

Sofia simply nodded towards her sister at her suggestion.

"Well, you two get the laptops out and look for flights, and Chris and I will sort the dishes and check on the girls," instructed Isabella, taking control.

An hour or so later, and with flights booked, Sofia decided to call Sister Lucianna and tell her about the plans they had made. Before concluding the conversation, she once again asked about Diego, but there was no real change in his condition.

"We are on the fifth floor," Lucianna advised. "*Me asegurare de que este aqui cuando vengas* [I will make sure I am here when you come]," she added.

The following afternoon Sofia and Maria were making their way to Manchester Airport. Chris couldn't help wondering how many more times he would have to make this trip, although this flight to Bogotá was from Manchester (not like previous ones, from Gatwick), which was a great help. Flights were on time according to the flight information. The sisters made their way towards the boarding gate and their long trip to Colombia.

Chris on the other hand found himself pulling into his driveway an hour and a half later to be greeted with a warm smile and a cup of coffee.

"All went smoothly," he offered as he sat down with Isabella on the settee to sort out a routine between them, discussing school runs and work at Aroma.

The hours ticked by on the long-distance flight, and Sofia and Maria cuddled into each other for comfort, not of course knowing what they might find when they got to the hospital. Having surprisingly slept for a few hours, it did not seem long before the 747 was making its approach into Bogotá. As it came in to land and then taxi towards a gate, Sofia nervously reminded Maria about the passport history she had had to encounter over the past few years flying in and out of Bogotá.

Nodding, Maria just simply said, "Don't worry. Leave it to me. Use your passport now."

As they made their way to passport control, having claimed their baggage, a queue was forming, making Sofia rather edgy.

'Surely nothing can hold us up on such an important visit, can it?' she thought.

As predicted, Maria and Sofia slipped through passport control very quickly, hailed a taxi and were on their way to the hospital.

"How did we get through that quickly, Maria?" enquired Sofia.

"I'll tell you more later," she replied. "Let's just say Juan is a distant friend of mine, and he owes me a favour."

As the taxi eased its way through the traffic, the sisters had no idea what was in store for them at the hospital – or in fact where they would stay that night – but that at this moment was of secondary importance. The traffic was busy as late afternoon eased into early evening. It was hot and although Sofia was used to the heat in Bogotá, she now found herself shedding some clothes.

As the taxi eased to a stop outside the hospital entrance, glancing up at the hospital building Sofia frowned and muttered that everything had changed since she was last there. "How long has this unit been here?" she asked her sister.

Maria shrugged her shoulders. "I think it was finished in early 2019," she replied.

Like Sofia, Maria swallowed hard, and arm in arm they walked towards the reception area, where the lift would take them to the fifth floor. The lift rose smoothly, arriving at level five. The sisters found things a little different from how they had expected them to be with the staff wearing face masks. They were immediately stopped and handed masks to wear and requested to use the hand sanitisers. Frowning at this rather strange situation, they made their way to the nurses' station, where they asked to see Sister Lucianna.

A voice from behind them said hello. It was Lucianna. "I am pleased to meet you. Follow me, please."

She led them to a private room where they could talk.

In her limited English, Lucianna explained that Diego had come into hospital not feeling very well four days ago. His tumour had not reduced and on top of that he was finding it hard to breathe. He was now on a ventilator, having been diagnosed with Covid.

"Is that what all the masks and hand sanitiser is about?" asked Maria.

Lucianna nodded and briefly explained, and then added that there was no real positive news to report.

"Is he in a lot of pain?" asked Sofia.

Lucianna told them that his pain was being controlled, but he might only have forty-eight hours or so.

"So it was good that we came now," said Sofia.

Ten minutes later Maria and Sofia approached Diego's bed. He appeared to be asleep, but seemingly felt their presence and opened his eyes followed by a broad smile.

The sisters held his hand and drew some comfort when they twice heard him say in a weak voice, "Thank you." He then motioned to Sofia to open his bedside drawer and take a letter for them to read after they had left the hospital.

Outside in the evening sunshine, the girls sat on a bench and opened the note Diego had given them. It told them they could stay in his apartment and that more information would be there for them to read and deal with.

Shrugging her shoulders, Sofia said, "Well, let's go to the apartment and sort ourselves out. I am so glad we came."

Maria nodded and another taxi ride took them to Diego's five minutes later. As they entered the flat some letters could be seen on the table in front of them. Firstly, though, they decided to shower and freshen up. Soon after, Sofia was back at the table reading the notes Diego had left.

"Anything interesting?" asked Maria.

"By all accounts a Señor Ardillas will explain everything to us, and I think we have a surprise coming," suggested Sofia.

Maria started to read the notes too.

"Oh, my God!" was all Maria could muster as she started to cry, realising the extent of Diego's wishes.

"He knows he is near the end!" Sofia exclaimed. "Oh, and he wishes to be cremated, with half of his ashes being taken to

England and the remainder to Santander, when the time comes."

"He could have chosen somewhere nearer," Maria cheekily said with tears still rolling down her cheeks.

"I think I ought to give Chris and Isabella a call," suggested Sofia, making her way to the bedroom.

Phone call over, Maria asked if all was OK back home.

"Fine," Sofia said.

"What do we do now?" Maria quizzed Sofia.

"I think we need something to eat and bed," Sofia said.

Outside, they soon found a bar which offered some nice-smelling food, and that would do for now. Whilst enjoying their food, Sofia heard her phone ring.

"Who can that be?" she asked as she looked at the number illuminated. "It's not from home, so a local— Ah, the hospital! *Hola. Si . . . . Si,*" Sofia muttered and switched off the phone.

"What is it?" Maria anxiously asked.

"It was the hospital . . . . Diego passed away thirty minutes ago. He was comfortable with little pain."

Sofia and Maria shed some tears, paid the bill and made their way outside for fresh air and a walk towards the apartment.

"Well, we didn't get very far with our plan, did we?" Maria said, sniffing and trying to lift the mood.

Having arrived back in the flat, Sofia thought she needed to call Chris to tell him the very latest news about Diego. Five minutes or so later they were sat on the settee trying to make sense of the last few hours. Some sleep was called for, although that might be difficult, but they needed rest of some sort so they could face the following day.

Waking early to beautiful sunshine, Sofia slipped into the dining area and tried to make sense of the letter Diego had left them. Obviously the lawyer, Señor Ardillas, would explain all, so a call to him would be first.

'We are the next of kin,' she thought, 'but what will that entail?' she asked herself.

Maria then appeared from the bedroom and Sofia then talked a few things through with her. Diego's affairs were, it appeared, simple, with only three people involved, but Señor Ardillas, at the law firm Martinez and Garcia, would confirm everything.

"Where are they?" asked Maria.

"Apparently a few minutes' walk from here," confirmed Sofia.

Later that morning, having collected a death certificate from the hospital, and having thanked Sister Lucianna for the care they had given Diego, their next stop was to Martinez and Garcia for a meeting with Señor Ardillas, who would explain about Diego's will and his wishes. As the church clock chimed eleven o'clock they arrived in the reception area and asked for Señor Ardillas. Minutes later he came and met them and guided them to his office, where he extended his condolences.

"He was a lovely man, your Uncle Diego," he added.

Agreeing, both the girls sat on the settee, providing some comfort for what they were about to hear.

"I am not sure how much you know about your uncle's finances, so perhaps I should briefly explain a few things," he said. "Diego, many, many years ago invested some money in the Emerald Stone Company in Santander. When he realised six months or so ago he really was not well with his cancer, he sold his share to the other directors of ESC. Of course the gems are worth considerably more now than all those years ago, so Diego's decision to invest was an excellent one, as you will see in these documents. You must take them away, read and sign them, and then return them to me. You both are now co-owners of Diego's apartment, and he also owned three others there, which of course you also now own, Maria!"

"What, me?" she exclaimed.

"Yes, you," said Señor Ardillas. "This will give you security and a regular income. Sofia, you will I am sure be pleased with this document, which simply confirms you now own the freehold to Nottingham 26. Diego wanted you to have that security for the future. Also in this package are other personal things which you will understand when you see them. This also includes your cousin Isabella."

An hour or so later they were out in the sunshine again, holding a large padded envelope containing several documents. Surprised by the events of the past hour, they made their way back to the apartment, where they could absorb what they had been told, and prepare themselves for what could be life-changing circumstances. As they arrived back at the apartment, Maria, spotting a bar, told Sofia to go on upstairs and she would follow in a couple of minutes. Opening the apartment door, Sofia switched on the kettle and sat down on a chair.

"You crafty old fox, Diego!" she muttered.

With that, Maria came back, closed the door and started to open a bottle of champagne.

"This is a sad occasion," she said, "but it sounds like Diego wants us to live and have fun, so fun we will have."

Agreeing, Sofia fetched two glasses and slowly they started to smile and enjoy the delights of the bottle.

As the afternoon progressed they made attempts to understand the papers they'd been given, and this was before they opened the package. It was now late afternoon and following a doze (champagne!) Sofia then decided to open the padded envelope, which contained three pouches. Suddenly she was in a state of déjà vu.

'I have been here before,' she thought.

Several large emeralds appeared, and she knew that they were valuable. Coming into the room, Maria was passed her pouch, and immediately realised what was going on.

"Oh, my God!" she said as she sat down and faced her sister. "I never realised that Diego was such a wealthy man, did you?"

"Well, I knew he bought into the emerald business in Santander many years ago, but I had no idea to what extent he was involved," added Sofia. "We all seem to have been given something to secure our futures," Sofia outlined, "which is wonderful," she added.

"We need to sign all this and get it back to Señor Ardillas," urged Maria, who could not quite believe what had happened.

"I need to go back home, Maria," sighed Sofia.

Nodding in agreement, Maria added that she too needed to go back to work at Medellín. However, now being a property owner she thought she would seek a transfer to Bogotá, where she could keep an eye on her assets. "One question," Maria queried: "how on earth are you going to get those emeralds through customs?"

Smiling, Sofia had a good idea.

Having now booked her flight back home, and having phoned Chris to tell him what she had arranged, Sofia spent the last few hours of her time in Colombia reminiscing over the years she had spent with Uncle Diego discussing plans and the future, which now looked quite rosy. She was very sad, but happy to be going home (although not directly) to Chris and her girls, whom she had missed greatly.

The following morning Sofia and Maria shared a taxi to the airport, where flights to Medellín were quite regular. Sofia on the other hand would have to wait awhile for hers. Once again Sofia nervously waited to pass through passport control. She had prepared her make-up, looking totally distraught, put on some dark glasses and a scarf over her head, and was looking very much like a grieving widow. Maria watched in case she was needed, although what could she really do if Sofia was stopped? However, after explaining about the urn and the ashes of her uncle she was allowed to pass through into the departure area. Here she waited for Maria.

The two sisters briefly met up again, and Maria gasped, "How did you do that?"

"Do what?" Sofia replied.

"Carry that off. What did you do with the gems?" Maria continued, anxious to know.

Smiling, Sofia whispered, "Diego would want some company on my long flight home."

Maria and Sofia hugged for the final time and made their way to their respective boarding gates, safe in the knowledge that Diego would always be with them in some form.

A few hours later Maria had arrived back in Medellín. She collected her car and drove the short distance to her apartment. Following some refreshment, she sat and considered what the past few days with her sister had produced under sad circumstances. She was now the owner of three apartments in Bogotá, and this would give her an income. However, she also realised that she would have to maintain them also. What should she do, and what was the best way forward? 'Time to think about the future,' she thought.

In mid-air Sofia, with the urn tucked tightly into her side, had fallen asleep whilst thinking about her gift from Diego's will. Martyn van Bastin, Diego's long time-friend in Amsterdam, would help her turn the emeralds into cash for her to invest somewhere, sometime. Her phone call to Chris the night before was not an easy one, especially when she said she was flying to Amsterdam first. He would of course understand when she told him the complete story.

Hours later Sofia, making her way out of Schiphol Airport, heard a voice shouting to her. As she turned around she realised it was Martyn.

"Hello. Good to see you," he said excitedly.

"Hi," said Sofia.

Walking towards the car, Martyn expressed how sad he was to hear about his dear friend Diego.

"I will tell you more later," she said.

Martyn drove the few miles to his house just outside the city.

"Can I offer you a drink of any kind?" asked Martyn.

"Thank you – just a coffee," replied Sofia, who was by now hungry and tired. Taking a sip of her much needed drink, Sofia settled to explain everything to Martyn. "Diego died ten days ago," said Sofia. She went on to explain how, why and where.

She passed on a letter that Diego had written to his dear friend, which Martyn read intently. When he had finished reading, Sofia eased the small urn out of her travel bag and a much surprised Martyn, with mouth wide open, wondered what on earth Sofia was doing. Sofia smiled, opened the urn and pulled out a pouch with the emeralds inside.

"Would you value these for me? They are my inheritance," she explained.

Smiling to himself now, Martyn nodded and said of course he would.

Following a good night's sleep, Martyn and Sofia made their way into the city of Amsterdam, and visited Martyn's office. An hour or so later, the answer!

"OK, are you ready for this?" Martyn enquired.

Sofia smiled and in a relaxed mood waited for Martyn's report on the value of the gemstones in his hand.

"Today, and I will quote you in English pounds, these are valued at approximately £120–150,000. I could have a buyer within an hour or so, and the money transferred to your bank account in the UK later today."

Sofia remained sat in the chair, thinking that if she got up she might fall down with shock.

"Are you serious?" she asked.

"Excuse the pun – deadly," replied Martyn. "They are some of the best-quality emeralds I have seen in years," he added.

"You will take a healthy commission, won't you?" Sofia enquired.

"No. Diego was a very dear friend, so . . ."

Sofia then insisted he take an extra percentage as it would be what Diego would want. With that, he agreed.

A BA flight was available at seven o'clock that evening, and Sofia anxiously wanted to get back home to Chris and the girls, whom she had missed so much. Floating through the airport towards the boarding gate, Sofia had a very warm feeling inside her. True she had lost her Uncle Diego, to whom she owed so much – after all, Aroma would not have existed if it was not for him – but now she could look with huge confidence at her bank account. She could now ease away any problems they might have, and plan a very healthy future that would not have been possible before.

East Midlands Airport was quiet when Sofia arrived, and there was the man in her life waiting for her.

"Would you be Sofia Dobson?" Chris asked.

As they hugged each other, she said, "I certainly am, and it's so good to be home."

The drive from the airport to home was not long, and Chris realised that Sofia was tired; so he did not bombard her with questions, yet. Fortunately the children would be in bed fast asleep, so Sofia had only Isabella to face – and there was an envelope to give her too.

Sofia slumped into her chair, and with a very large glass of Chardonnay in hand she started to tell Chris and Isabella the story of her past and her last visit to Colombia. After explaining everything, Sofia then reached into her handbag exposing not only the urn containing Diego's ashes, but a much used passport, which she passed to Isabella.

"Thank you for deputising for me. You have helped me many times to create a disguise for me getting in and out of Colombia – but no more," she said with a smile.

She then handed Isabella her letter, and then all three stood and raised a glass to Uncle Diego.

SCORNED EX-LOVER

The phone rang.

"Hello."

"Oh, hello. Mrs Johnson?"

"Yes."

"Oh, you don't know me. My name is Marilyn La Rue, and I thought you ought to know that I have been having an affair with your husband for the past six months or so. Rest assured it is all over now as I think he has moved on to a much younger model."

The call ended.

'What the hell was that!' Hilary Johnson thought. She could not believe what she had just heard. Was that right? No, it couldn't be. A tear or two started to trickle down her cheek, but that was quickly followed by a pang of rage and anger. 'Coffee,' she thought, 'yes, strong coffee!'

As she walked into the kitchen to switch on the kettle she grabbed her mobile and called her long-time friend Maggie, who lived three doors away.

Following the brief call for support, Maggie came around and Hilary relayed the phone call to her.

"Oh, my God!" said Maggie. "Do you believe her?"

"Of course I don't," Hilary replied. "But, in the short time since the call, and taking into account the smug and confident manner in which she delivered her message, I have begun to wonder."

"OK, now let us be logical here," stressed Maggie.

"Hold on!" Hilary interrupted. "I suppose Graham has been spending an awful lot of time away these past few months."

"Ah-ha," said her friend. "Nevertheless we still need to be

level-headed about all this, and not jump to any conclusions. How long have you two been married?" Maggie asked.

"Thirty years or so," Hilary answered.

"So you do not want to create a problem if there isn't one, do you?" her neighbour added.

"No, I do not," said Hilary emphatically.

Maggie was now deep in thought.

"What is it?" Hilary asked her friend. "You are up to something, I can tell."

"Well, we need to investigate this and make a plan. We need to see who Marilyn La Rue is, or if she exists at all," Maggie explained. "How about we go down to the bistro tonight – say, 7.30-ish – for a chat?"

After ordering two large glasses of Shiraz, the two women found a quiet corner table in the bistro where they could not be overheard. Maggie seemingly was in detective mode. She reached for a pen and a pad from her bag.

"If we are to save your marriage, Hilary, we need some facts," Maggie stated. "Before we start, is everything OK in the bedroom department?" she enquired.

"Of course, but Graham always seems too tired and uninterested and it is usually me that starts anything, if you know what I mean," confirmed Hilary.

Maggie started to scribble.

"Graham is a production manager with Pre-Cast Foundations?" Maggie asked.

Hilary just nodded.

"We need to establish where he goes every Monday, because if this La Rue women is telling the truth then their rendezvous point will surely be in the same vicinity, don't you think?" Maggie suggested.

"Makes sense," Hilary said.

"Do you know Graham's movements next week?" Maggie enquired.

"Only that he's away again," Hilary added miserably.

"Right – on Monday morning I suggest you call his office saying you need to get hold of Graham on a family matter, and ask where he is going so you can get in touch."

The ladies ordered another glass of wine, content in the knowledge that they had a plan in place, either to prove Miss La Rue to be a nasty, vindictive woman or to catch Graham out.

Maggie came around to Hilary on Monday morning, anxious to hear the result of the phone call Hilary made.

"Well," said Hilary, "it appears that he's been going to Rochester every week for the past four months or so, working in a temporary office owned by Costar Construction."

Maggie, in thinking mode, said, "Rochester – that is about sixty to seventy miles away. Let's try to get to the bottom of this. You pack an overnight bag, and I will be around in fifteen minutes to pick you up."

Hilary nodded and headed upstairs to pick up a few things for their trip of discovery.

When Maggie arrived back at her friend's house, Hilary said that she had established the postcode for Costar Construction so it could be fed into the satnav.

"That will be helpful," Maggie said.

The drive to Rochester was slow to start with, but improved once they had cleared Woking.

"What are your thoughts, Maggie?" asked Hilary.

"Well, firstly we locate Costar's office and see if Graham's car is in the car park. Before that, though, we need to ascertain if they have a Miss Marilyn La Rue working for them."

With that they settled down for the journey ahead of them.

An hour or so later they were approaching their destination, and immediately picked up the signs for Kirkby Trading Estate, the address for Costar Construction. Pulling over to the side of the road, they made a call and enquired about Marilyn La Rue. Maggie listened, and as Hilary put the phone down said, "Well?"

"Costar's does not have a Miss La Rue working for them, but they know of her. She works as a buyer for one of their suppliers – Techform," explained Hilary.

"So where do they hang out?" asked Maggie.

"They are on the Three Miles Industrial Estate, on the other side of town," confirmed Hilary.

Just as they were considering their next move, Hilary shouted, "There's Graham's car pulling into the car park."

"Oh, so it is," Maggie said. "We should wait a minute and see what happens next."

It was now approaching five o'clock and the two ladies were feeling tired and hungry as they had been waiting now for nearly an hour. Suddenly, though, both were alerted when they saw Graham walking towards his car, followed by a very attractive blonde young lady, five feet six in height, slim and wearing high heels. Hilary thought that she oozed sex appeal.

"That's it!" she exclaimed. "That's the reason for him playing away – she's gorgeous," she continued.

As the sexy blonde slipped into her Ford Focus, Maggie said, "Let's follow her and see what happens next."

Ten minutes later they again eased to the side of the road and watched the Ford Focus slip into a hotel car park next to Graham's BMW.

"What now?" asked Hilary.

"Well, some 300 yards back there was a Premier Inn. Let us see if they have a room for the night where we can decide our next move," Maggie suggested.

"Fine by me," Hilary agreed, despite her feeling and looking rather glum.

Room booked, and refreshing showers enjoyed, both ladies were hungry. They decided to find the restaurant and study the menu.

"I am going to walk up to the Hilton Express later and find out the names they booked in under," said Hilary.

"Suppose you are seen?" queried Maggie.

"I'll take that chance," said Hilary.

Following their meal, Hilary strolled to the Hilton Express and asked her questions before returning to Maggie.

Enquiringly Maggie looked at her friend.

"Bloody nerve! They have booked in as Mr and Mrs Johnson," Hilary stated, fuming and becoming rather tearful.

Maggie did her best to console her friend, and decided an early night might not be a bad idea.

Having slept well, Maggie and Hilary chatted over breakfast about the day ahead.

"So where do we go from here?" Hilary asked.

"Well, I think we should call Miss La Rue," suggested Maggie.

"Wha-a-a-a-at!" replied Hilary.

"Let's see what she has to say for herself. We have nothing to lose," Maggie suggested.

Techform was easy to find, but it was an understatement to say that they were nervous at the thought of walking into reception, let alone meeting Marilyn.

The receptionist smiled as they walked through the door. "Can I help you?" she asked.

"Good morning. Do you have a Marilyn La Rue working here? And if so, could I see her, please?" said Hilary.

"Who would be calling?" the receptionist asked.

"Oh, my name is Mrs Johnson," Hilary confirmed.

With bated breath they waited for a response.

"Miss La Rue will be with you shortly," the receptionist confirmed.

A couple of minutes later an authoritative voice said, "Mrs Johnson?"

"Yes, that's me," said Hilary.

"I am Marilyn La Rue. If you care to follow me, then we can have a private chat."

Maggie and Hilary followed.

Marilyn La Rue was a very attractive lady in her late forties. She was smartly dressed and Hilary thought her quite seductive in her manner.

"Look – firstly I apologise for the call. It really is not my style – but your husband played a dirty trick on us, promising us an order which would have kept twenty jobs going. Despite Techform agreeing to his price, he then gave the order to a competitor. Then, despite bedding me for the last few months, he has now taken up with a much younger model."

Hilary found herself saying, "Red Ford Focus, blonde hair, slim, etc., etc."

"Yes, that's her," acknowledged Marilyn. "How do you know that?"

"They booked into the Hilton Express last night," Maggie said.

"Oh, did they?" Marilyn said thoughtfully.

Hilary was feeling quite emotional, and blurted out that she and Graham were finished. "I've had enough," she said.

"I am sorry," Marilyn said again, "but if you need help catching your man with the young Miss Fleming, just say. I mean you could just confront him."

"Look – I should hate you – in fact, part of me does – but [thinking quickly] what had you in mind?"

During the next few minutes the three women hatched a plan. Marilyn called the hotel and booked a room for 1.30 p.m. – a time and place where she used to meet Graham. Then she called Graham and made arrangements with him.

"Are you happy about this, Hilary?" asked Maggie.

"Yes, I just want closure," Hilary admitted.

Marilyn, wearing a loose top and short skirt, opened the door of room 130 to receive Graham.

"So you have forgiven me," he said as he took off his jacket and loosened his tie, approaching Marilyn.

At that moment a voice coming from the bathroom said, "Hi, Graham."

As he turned around he saw Hilary.

"What the hell are you doing here?" he asked.

"Oh," she replied, "I've just been having a chat with one of your ex-mistresses about dropping her prices – or should I say *panties*? And your new young filly, Miss Fleming, has told us what you are like in bed," Hilary said.

With that the door opened and in walked Maggie.

"Ah, Graham, a little news: Miss Fleming did not know you were married, and therefore does not want to see you again," she stated.

"Neither do I," Marilyn added.

And finally Hilary added, "It's over, you bastard! Your things will be in the garage when you get back."

Once again Marilyn La Rue apologised to Hilary, who in turn thanked her for her help in confirming Graham's guilt. Feeling rather sad, Hilary and Maggie drove back to Woking. Her marriage was over, but a small consolation was that she had a very dear friend in Maggie, who would help her through the inevitable turmoil that lay ahead.

DIDN'T SEE THAT COMING

Jill was a bored housewife of fifty-two. She was very attractive with shoulder-length hair. She was five foot ten and had a really good figure. Her husband, Tom, worked away from home virtually all the time, just coming home at weekends. In fact over the past few years it was difficult to recall a time when he did work from home. His job was in engineering, which was stressful. Any suggestion that they move house nearer his place of work was always met with a blunt no!

Jill had a very lonely existence. True, she had plenty of money and drove a lovely top-of-the-range Lexus, which enabled her to get from A to B, but it didn't talk to her. She had been married to Tom for nearly thirty years and, although they were inseparable in the early part of their married life, Tom's interest became less and less towards Jill and more and more towards his work. Jill did think that perhaps Tom was having an affair and she thought about getting to the bottom of that theory, but she ignored it, hoping he would just come back to her.

At the gym, which Jill tried to visit twice a week, she met Tara, a young, vibrant slightly younger lady. In many respects she envied Tara as she seemed to have lots of friends. Of course as a reporter for the *County Weekly* she would naturally know a few people, but that only made things worse in a way as Jill did not work or have a network of friends.

With the weekend over, Tom loaded his suitcase, briefcase and laptop into the boot of his car, pecked his wife on her cheek and drove off into the sunset.

'Another agonising week of loneliness and no affection.' she thought. 'Who ever pays me any attention and gives me any love?'

Oh, she usually had a few whistles from the builders on the high-rise development in the town, but it was not the same. This did make her smile, but it was no substitute for real affection.

Thankfully it was a gym day, and after a shower Jill drove the couple or so miles into town and prepared herself for an hour or so of physical exercise. Tara ended up being next to her when they were doing floor exercises, and in a moment of non-activity they arranged to go out for coffee after the gym.

The Express Coffee Bar, just off the High Street, was quite busy, but they did manage to find a couple of seats towards the back of the shop, and there they settled in for a long chat. The longer their chat went on, the more Jill felt good and thought what a caring person Tara seemed. When they came to say goodbye Tara invited Jill over for an evening meal at her apartment. Jill was thrilled at this opportunity to hopefully solidify a friendship.

Thursday evening came, and at 6.30 p.m. Jill knocked on the door of Tara's apartment.

Opening the door with a broad smile, Tara welcomed Jill, saying, "You look lovely."

"Thank you," said Jill. "May I say that you look very nice too."

"That's nice. What would you like to drink?" Tara asked.

"Oh, a G & T, please," replied Jill.

Drinks in hand, they made themselves comfortable and chatted about anything and everything for about twenty minutes whilst the casserole was cooking.

The evening progressed with Jill feeling more and more relaxed in Tara's company. Not having felt kindness and affection for some time, it was a surprise to feel just that from Tara, whom she seemed to be having feelings for. A lovely evening was coming to an end and it was time to go.

As she was putting her coat on, Tara gave Jill a peck on the cheek and said, "Thanks for coming."

With that they moved to the door and, without thinking, Jill kissed Tara on the lips.

"Oh, I am sorry," Jill said, rather embarrassed.

Tara just smiled. "Please don't be. I wanted to do that indoors," she said. "But thank you. I have had feelings for you for a few weeks now," she explained.

"I thought you were married," said Jill.

"Oh, good God, no!" confirmed Tara. "But you are," Tara stated.

"Yes, but I get little or no love or affection at home. That is why this evening has been great," Jill said.

They said their goodnights and Jill left for home.

Jill drove the short distance home feeling somewhat elated with her evening out, and the time spent with her new girlfriend. Friday evening would soon be here and coldness would soon return.

'Roll on Monday!' she thought.

Tara had had a lesbian relationship before, but it sadly ended after six months when her current job cropped up and she had to move the 100 or so miles to take up the offer. She had found Jill a person she could get close to. She enjoyed her company and thought there might be a future for them together. Tara had also had relationships with men, but they were more off than on.

Steph, Jill's sister, lived in Devon and tried supporting her on the phone because she could not be there with her that often. However, Steph thought it time to see her younger sister in Leicester and called to invite herself to the East Midlands. Jill was thrilled, and made preparations for her visit at the end of the month.

Monday morning came and Jill was surprised to find Tom still in the house.

"What is going on?" she enquired. "Why are you still here?" she asked.

"I am about to be offered a new job in Grangemouth, Scotland. It is a promotion, and I am awaiting confirmation," he said.

"So will you be away all the time?" she asked.

"Well, yes," he confirmed. "But you can come with me if you like," Tom suggested.

"Not bloody likely!" she angrily told him. "In all the years I have offered to move nearer your work to help, you have always said no, so my answer emphatically is no, no, no," Jill raged.

With that the phone rang. Jill answered it and passed it to Tom.

Ten minutes later Tom confirmed that that was confirmation of the job, which would start in two weeks.

Jill exploded: "You selfish bastard!" she cried.

With that, Tom gathered his things together.

Jill, though, was not finished: "I think we should sell this house, share the proceeds and move on," she suggested.

"OK, if that is what you want," said Tom, and out to the car he went.

Within a few minutes he was gone.

Jill was now in tears and so angry. She picked up the phone and called her new friend, Tara.

"Are you OK?" Tara asked.

"No, not really," replied Jill. "Can you come over?" she pleaded.

"I'll be there in fifteen minutes," she confirmed.

Jill was still very upset when Tara came around, but settled down when given a warm hug by Tara. Jill felt warm and reassured by her presence – so much so that a few tender kisses followed. At this point Tara thought to put her cards on the table, and with coffee in hand explained about her sexual preferences. Looking at Jill, she was surprised that she was smiling.

"What?" she asked.

Jill continued to smile, then said, "Does that matter? If you want me, that's fine. I want you, so what is the problem? Let's take it slowly and see what happens," she continued.

Looking at her watch, Tara said she had to go as she had a meeting which she could not miss. But "I will be back by three," she confirmed.

"That's fine," said Jill. "See you later."

It was late in the afternoon when Tara drove back to see Jill, who by now was feeling much better. They chatted freely with each other and had an enjoyable evening going over a few things, and enjoying a glass or two of cold Pinot. However, this led both of them to completely lose all their inhibitions, and they found themselves making love. Feeling fulfilled from this experience, they just cuddled each other into the night. It was the first time Jill had felt love and tenderness in a very long time.

Tara stayed until morning, but left early for work. Jill, excited by the events of the last few hours, was surprised when the phone rang. The agent she had called said he would like to come over that morning, as he might have a potential buyer, despite not yet having seen the property. She agreed and had a quick tidy.

Two hours later, and with the agent pleased with what he had seen, he called again to ask if he could bring the couple around. Again Jill agreed. By teatime that day Jill had received an offer which was close to the asking price. Now she had to call Tom and tell him – not a call she wanted to make. She also had to tell him that her sister was coming to stay, and that would probably mean that he would not come home that weekend.

'Good,' she thought.

The sisters greeted each other warmly and soon, with coffee in hand, settled down to update each other on their respective lives. Steph's life seemed so calm and interesting, with friends to share things with.

After ten minutes or so Steph said, "OK, that's me; now, what about you?"

With that, Jill broke down and cried in her sister's arms.

"Oh dear – that bad, eh?" Steph said. For the next half an hour Jill offloaded everything, which brought Steph to say, "I am coming to see you more often; you can't go on like this. It sounds as though you may have found a friend in Tara, though. It's not quite what I expected from my sister, but what the hell!"

Ten Weeks Later

With the paperwork completed, Jill was almost ready to move into her flat, which she had agreed to rent for twelve months.

'What a lovely thought: my very own place!'

With that the phone rang. It was Tara.

"Could we meet for a coffee?"

The Percolator Coffee Shop was quite quiet, so they found a table easily. Tara seemed worried about something and Jill thought she was not going to like whatever Tara was about to tell her.

"I have been offered another job – well, it is a promotion really. The *County Weekly* Group have realised that I am good at what I do and want me to fill a vacancy in our north-east office near Newcastle."

Surprised, shocked and with loads of mixed emotions, Jill asked Tara the all-important question of when?

"Three weeks," Tara said.

Jill felt this was a real body blow, but as she was about to say something she noticed Tara had a smile on her face.

"You could come with me," she said.

Jill said she needed to get her divorce sorted, plus speak to Mr Norris about the flat, and then perhaps they could talk again.

During the next three weeks Tara was a regular at Jill's, and her visits were always a joyous affair.

A Few Weeks Later

The divorce proceedings were nearly complete. Jill had spoken to Mr Norris, who agreed to leave the term of rent flexible. With the house sold and the divorce almost done, Jill felt better than she had done for years. She thought her problems were behind her.

Enjoying her new book, one day Jill was surprised to have a phone call so late in the evening.

"Hi, Jill."

It was Tara.

"Hello. How lovely to hear you! How are things?"

"Going well actually. It is quite nice here and the people are very friendly. Listen – I was wondering if you would like to come up for the weekend?"

How could Jill say no?

"That would be good. Send me directions and I will drive up on Friday morning."

"OK, then we can talk about a few things," said Tara. "I am off out to cover a story. See you on Friday," she continued.

"Bye," said Jill, for some reason not totally convinced about a few things and the way they were said.

However, Newcastle here we come!

Realising that this was a difficult time, Steph decided to come and stay with her sister.

"Are you sure about moving in with Tara?" Steph asked.

"Why do you ask?" Jill asked.

"You have not known her that long – you have just about divorced Tom, and I don't want you to get hurt again," explained Steph.

"Yes, I suppose it is a bit quick," Jill admitted.

"Keep hold of your new flat and take your time deciding," Steph advised. "I'll go up with you to Newcastle for the weekend if you would like. Don't worry – I won't cramp your style. In fact I'll stay in a Premier Inn close by," she offered.

"That would be lovely," Jill said.

Tara was completely surprised to see Jill with another woman, but was reassured when Jill introduced Steph as her sister.

"Don't worry as Steph is—"

"I'm here to see some friends," Steph said.

"Yes," added Jill, frowning at her sister.

Sunday afternoon came all too soon, and it seemed that Steph wanted them to go quickly to the car and drive away.

"What's the rush?" asked Jill. "And where are we going?" she added.

"Did Tara go out this morning for a paper or . . . ?" asked Steph.

"Yes, she did. Why?"

"She was gone for about an hour, yes?" Steph asked.

"Yes. What is this?" asked Jill.

Steph was suspicious of Tara. She had no idea why, but did not want to see her sister ripped off as she had been hurt enough. She had watched Tara leave her flat, and followed her. In a nearby coffee bar she had met a man – not any man, but Tom. Now, how did all this tie up? Their greeting was like that of a married couple and it started Steph thinking. Now she outlined her story to Jill.

"What!" exclaimed Jill. "Are you serious?" she added.

"Sure am," said Steph. "We need to do some serious investigation," suggested Steph.

Jill was still asleep in the Premier Inn, but Steph had been on the phone to the editor of the *County Weekly* and to the Public Record Office. She had also contacted Tom's office, and spoken to his boss at Eden Engineering. Having come back to their room, Steph sat on the bed and told Jill her findings.

"OK, here we go. Firstly, has your divorce actually gone through yet?"

Jill replied, "No, I am still waiting for the final papers to come back from Tom."

"Well, your girlfriend has asked for this move to be near her (wait for it) new husband of six months. The records show that Tara and Tom were married at Bicester Registry Office on the 4th of April. Tom did not get promotion, but was moved – he cocked up a job and the company moved him away. The vitally important bit, though, is for you to call your solicitor now. Your ex could be a bigamist."

Jill called Smyth, Jones & Hilter, and five minutes later Jill confirmed that, no, the divorce had not gone through yet.

"What the hell do we do now?" asked Jill.

"Hold on to your flat and start a new life," suggested Steph, and come back to Devon with me for a while.

"Why?" asked Jill. "Why any of this?" she asked again.

"Underneath, Tara is a very unsure person. She seeks attention and falls in love easily. She met Tom on his last project and the rest is history."

"How do you know all this?" asked Jill.

With some hesitation, Steph said, "Well, history has a habit of repeating itself sometimes. Then throw in a few coincidences, and bingo!"

"I'm not sure what you mean," said Jill.

"I know Tara. She tried it on with me when she was working in Honiton. It began as a chat about the county show. Things did not develop, though. That girl can be trouble with a capital T."

"So what do we do now?"

"Apart from driving back to Devon, I think you should just make a call and let Tom and Tara deal with it."

THE PROFESSIONAL MOURNERS

'Earth to earth, ashes to ashes, dust to dust' was the phrase which stuck in Geoff's mind following the funeral service of his friend Tom. It was an unexpected death. Tom always seemed fit and healthy, playing lots of sport, and he had been a postman in the town for the past fifteen years or so.

"So why?" Geoff asked himself.

He had not been in touch with Tom for a few months due to work commitments, and this made Geoff feel a little embarrassed and awkward approaching Jilly, Tom's wife. However, he did briefly have a few words with her, which eased his feeling of guilt. Jilly made it clear, though, that she would like him to come to the wake, which was being held at the Royal Oak, three miles outside town – a place she and Tom used to frequent. Geoff was happy to say he would.

Walking back to his car, Geoff kept thinking about how such a fit person as Tom could die so relatively young. Perhaps in the following few hours he might find out. As he drove the few miles out of town, Geoff's mind drifted to his own health and fitness. He considered that all the driving he was doing could not help – but he couldn't easily change jobs! He had stopped going to five-a-side and jogging, as he usually came home from work completely worn out.

Geoff walked into the pub and found it very busy, mainly due to the mourners from the nearby funeral service.

"Hi, Geoff," a voice called out.

"Well, well, well," said Geoff, "Dave Constance – and your lovely lady, Monica. How are you?"

"We are fine, thank you," said Dave.

Whilst Geoff was giving Monica a peck on the cheek, Dave said, "Let me buy you a drink. A pint?"

"Oh, yes, please," said Geoff.

Jilly was of course doing the rounds, but she soon came over to the three friends.

"Thank you so much for coming," she said.

"No problem," said Monica.

Looking a little tearful, Jilly then made her way back towards the ladies.

"It's very sad, isn't it?" said Geoff.

"Indeed it is," added Dave.

"Tell me: what was it that . . . ?"

"Killed him," said Dave.

"Yes," confirmed Geoff.

"Bowel cancer," replied Dave.

"Bloody hell!" said Geoff rather loudly, and the chat then continued.

Three Hours Later

Dave and Monica started to make their way out of the Royal Oak towards the car park, having said their goodbyes to both Jilly and Geoff. There was most certainly an air of sadness as they drove home, and for Geoff it was time to reflect on his life too.

As soon as he arrived home he picked up the phone and arranged a game of golf with his mates on Sunday. He also couldn't help thinking about the superb spread of food laid on at the Royal Oak. Jilly had done Tom proud as far as that was concerned.

Winning his game of golf on Sunday certainly cheered Geoff up.

However, as the four friends sat down for a well-earned drink, Harold, the oldest of the group, asked, "Did you hear the sad news about Cyril Martin?"

"No," they chorused.

"Well, he passed away last Thursday aged eighty-four. He was club captain five years ago – lovely man."

"When's the funeral?" asked Geoff.

Harold took a sip of his drink and then said, "Three weeks yesterday, at St Martin's Church, and the wake is in the Barton Hotel, across the road."

The others agreed they would try to be there.

Three Weeks Later

The church was full for the funeral of Cyril, a well-respected gentleman, and a man who would be sadly missed. After the service mourners poured into the Barton Hotel conference hall, where after a few words a finger buffet was served. Geoff did not feel so sad as he did at Tom's funeral, and he started to enjoy the lovely spread of food.

Moving around the masses, Geoff bumped into a couple of Cyril's relatives who had come down from Wellington, in Somerset. After talking for what seemed like ages, Geoff moved on and started a conversation with a rather attractive lady – a granddaughter of Cyril. Eve had a naughty sense of humour, which Geoff liked, and for nearly an hour they chatted. The result of this was the exchanging of addresses and phone numbers. Eve, like Geoff, was single and very much up for some fun, despite the sad event they were attending.

Nine o'Clock That Night

Geoff's phone rang and to his surprise it was Eve.

"Hi. What are you doing?" she asked.

"Well, nothing very much. Why?" he answered.

"Fancy a drink?" asked Eve.

"Yeah, but where?" said Geoff.

"Your area," said Eve.

"OK, meet me at the Corner Inn, in the square, in about fifteen minutes," suggested Geoff.

"Fine," said Eve.

After a quick spray of deodorant and a comb through his hair he walked towards the pub to meet Eve.

'Oh, my God,' he thought as he opened the lounge-bar door. Eve was smiling and looking vastly different from her appearance at the funeral. From that moment they never stopped talking, and a mutual feeling grew between them. Eve and Geoff decided to meet for lunch the following day, before she had to catch the train back to Taunton.

Sunday Lunchtime

Geoff picked up Eve at the hotel and drove to the Goose and Feather, a country pub just outside the town, where they enjoyed a really lovely roast lunch together. During this time Geoff sensed a question coming from Eve, and then suddenly she asked the question he was half expecting.

"Tell me: is this goodbye today, or do you want to meet up again and let things develop?"

Geoff pondered over that question for about two seconds.

"I would like very much for it to continue," he said.

Then he posed a question of his own: "I have to go to Bristol tomorrow. Why don't I drive you home?"

Eve nodded enthusiastically. "There is one problem though," she said.

"Oh?" said Geoff.

"I have already booked out of the hotel, so I have no room for the night."

Not wishing to appear too keen, he said, "I have a spare bed at my place if you like."

"Deal," she said with a smile. "That would be lovely if you are sure."

"You bet!" said Geoff.

The drive up the motorway the following morning was uneventful, allowing plenty of discussion about their future relationship.

Out of the blue Eve said, "Oh, I have just remembered I have another bloody funeral to go to, tomorrow, and I don't know anyone who will be there."

"What time tomorrow?" asked Geoff.

"Oh, 2 p.m., I think. Why?" enquired Eve.

"I'll go with you if that would help," suggested Geoff.

"If you are sure, you're on," said Eve. "Will you have to rush home after?" she tongue-in-cheek asked.

"Not at all," confirmed Geoff.

"Oh, good," said Eve as they pulled into Harvest Moon Drive and stopped outside number 22.

Twenty-Four Hours Later

Entering St Mark's Church, Eve and Geoff held hands as if they were a married couple. As neither of them knew anybody there, what harm would it do?

At four o'clock in the Olde Lantern pub, Eve and Geoff were mingling with the other mourners when a voice said, "How are you connected to the deceased?"

"Who, me?" said Eve.

"Yes," said the man.

"Well, dear old Patrick used to teach me history and maths at the county grammar school," replied Eve.

"Pardon?" said the man. "I think not. George Stubbings was a very well-established builder, and never taught at any grammar school."

Dumbfounded, Eve looked at Geoff, who had just returned to her with another plateful of food. She did not know whether to laugh or cry.

"What's up?" asked Geoff.

"Oh, nothing really. We've only come to the wrong bloody funeral!"

At this point they started laughing uncontrollably.

Geoff and Eve's relationship grew and grew, and they often laughed at the incident at the Olde Lantern pub.

"Tell you what: I quite like this wake lark," said Geoff. "I'm not so sure about the funeral bit, but the food is usually superb, and you don't then have to get a meal when you get back," he added.

"So the moral of this is . . . ?" asked Eve.

"Well, we could try a few more and just pretend," suggested Geoff.

Three Months Later

"There it is – St Nicholas the Traveller. What a lovely church!" said Geoff.

"OK, now whose funeral is this?" asked Eve.

This was their tenth funeral in six months and they at least had learnt to gather some basic facts about the deceased beforehand.

"She is Mary Alton, aged seventy-seven, former head girl at the local school, and later in life she became the Lady Mayor of Hambrook," said Eve.

"Are we related in any way?" asked Geoff.

"Oh, my God, no. Let's just wing it after that," urged Eve.

The service was quite a sombre affair with a few tears being shed. After an hour mourners left the church and made their way towards the Flag and Whistle, in the High Street.

Eve and Geoff, hand in hand, strolled along and, like others, grabbed food and drinks on arrival at the pub. It was quite full, as expected by the number of people in the church.

Suddenly a voice spoke to them: "How are you connected to the deceased?"

When Eve and Geoff turned around they realised it was the same man who had approached them in the Olde Lantern pub several weeks previously.

"Well," said Eve, "we could ask you the same question."

Taking what seemed several minutes to answer, he said, "I've no connection whatsoever. I just like attending wakes. This is my sixteenth this year."

"How many?" Geoff exclaimed.

"Sixteenth," said the man.

All three looked at each other and started to laugh.

When they calmed down a little, Geoff said, "So you are what might be called a professional mourner."

Considering his reply, the man said, "Yes, I suppose you could say that."

"So," Eve added, "where and when is your next one?"

"Ah, that is at St Peter's Catholic Church in Hungerford in two weeks' time; the wake is to be at the Burford Arms. I should do some homework on it though, as it's a bit upmarket, if you get my drift," said the man.

Eve looked at Geoff and said to the man, "See you there, then."

They all chuckled as they made their way back towards the car park.

On approaching the car Geoff eyed a bench and suggested that they sit for a moment. A couple of minutes passed by and Geoff nervously reached into his pocket and pulled out a little box, which he opened and, on giving it to Eve, he proposed. All that could be heard was "Yes, yes, yes!" And hugs and kisses followed.

They drove back to Taunton happy in the knowledge that they had a long way to go, to becoming professional mourners.

Some who may read these stories may stumble across a piece of information or two that may not be completely accurate. Mistakes there may be, but remember I have written this for fun!